LACKAWANNA

LACKAWANNA

A NOVEL BY

Chester Aaron

J. B. LIPPINCOTT New York

Lackawanna

 Printed in the United States of America. For information address J. B. Lippincott Junior Books, 10 East 53rd Street, New York, N.Y. 10022. Published simultaneously in Canada by Fitzhenry & Whiteside Limited, Toronto.

Designed by Joyce Hopkins

1 2 3 4 5 6 7 8 9 10

First Edition

Library of Congress Cataloging in Publication Data

Aaron, Chester.

Lackawanna.

Summary: A gang of abandoned children, who christen themselves Lackawanna, live together during the Depression in order to survive and are galvanized into action when a hobo kidnaps one of its members.

[1. Depressions—1929—Fiction. 2. Kidnapping—Fiction.] I. Title.

PZ7.A12Lac 1986 [Fic] 83-47667

ISBN 0-397-32057-4

ISBN 0-397-32058-2 (lib. bdg.)

Two men have taught me trust, strength and love:

my brother Ray and Richard Lillard.
This novel is dedicated to them.

We did not dare to breathe a prayer,
Or to give our anguish scope:
Something was dead in each of us,
And what was dead was Hope.

Oscar Wilde
The Ballad of Reading Gaol

Contents

I

Prologue

Prologue

October. I run the whole way home, my spelling test, with Miss Guthrie's note—"Every word spelled correctly, Willy."—folded carefully and tucked safely in my shirt pocket. I search out mounds of aromatic maple leaves to roll in, to lie in without moving. I hold my breath and listen to the wind in the almost bare branches. When I breathe again, the aromas of autumn promise winter. Winter means Christmas.

Up and running, swinging my books at the end of a belt, I can see my father raking leaves, pulling them onto a pile already burning near the curb. We live in a house. Most of the other people in Flatbush live in apartments. At almost every curb throughout Brooklyn, supers, who take care of the apartment buildings, and fathers who live in houses, are burning leaves, as if autumn will refuse to complete its cycle unless that crisp, tangy scent is there to urge it on.

On every street all over Brooklyn, wherever there are trees, children are running home this Friday night, already anticipating Halloween, already tasting Thanksgiving turkey.

My father sees me coming, waves, and then, knowing his performance will delight me, pantomimes a soldier on guard duty, the rake-rifle at his shoulder, his puppetlike steps a parody of a disciplined soldier.

A framed photograph of my father stands on my mother's dressing table. My father in the photograph resembles my older brother, Ward. In 1917, when I was two years old and Ward was nine, my father volunteered to fight in Germany against the Kaiser. The Great War, the War to End All Wars, the War to Save Democracy. When using the words, my father always chuckles.

What did he know when he was urged to save democracy? He was young. Young people have ideals. On rainy weekends when I had to stay in the house, I'd sit on my parents' bed and wonder what it must be like to be grown up and in a war. There was that man, my father, a soldier in a wide-brimmed hat and a tight uniform. Lean, strong, a man who feared nothing. No problem, no villain, was too big, too complex, to conquer.

This day, in the street in front of our house, Ward and several other young men are passing a football. They take turns running out for passes, leaping high to grab the ball, dashing down the street, breaking free of imagined tacklers, crossing imagined goal lines, waving acknowledgment to the roars of imagined crowds.

Ward and my father, home from the warehouse, have bathed and changed clothes. Girls and older women, in their sweaters and jackets, play in the streets or sit on the stoops or just saunter along the sidewalks, soaking up the red-orange dusk.

I run through a final mound of leaves and, like a canny halfback, shift and skip to outmaneuver my stern soldier-father, to dodge a playful slap on the rump.

I burst into the house, rush down the hall to change clothes so I can join the big guys, Ward and the others, in their huddles in the street. Once inside, I have no choice but to stop. Supper is on the stove. Loaves of freshly baked bread under orange-brown crusts steam on the sink counter. Three apple pies follow their leader along the windowsill. My mother, cheeks red, stops just long enough, in the midst of her chores, to throw me a kiss, to call (to sing! she never just talks, she sings!), to sing a greeting that promises love and joy eternal.

I unbutton my corduroy knickers at the knee, untie my school shoes, pull off my long black stockings, and hop about in search of play clothes. Darkness is spreading across the skies. I have to hurry if I am to collect a few minutes of fun.

Apparently everyone in Brooklyn, in New York, in the United States, in the world, in the universe, is celebrating this midautumn evening.

Headline, *The New York Times*, Wednesday, October 30, 1929:

STOCK MARKET PLUNGES!

No fathers stand at the curbs tending piles of smoking leaves now. Tidy sidewalks and streets are no longer important. And in the kitchens the ovens are cold. I, as well as my friends, do not run to school; we walk, as if our country's tragedy requires mourning. Faces in the playground, in the streets, at home, are pale, frightened. The footballs in Brooklyn lie deflated in the corners of dark closets.

There are no jobs.

"Not just in Brooklyn," Ward says. "And not just in New York."

My father nods agreement. "All over the country." There is a suggestion of fear in those eyes that had, a mere twelve years ago, stared back in contempt at the face of war.

Ward and my father are home much of each day because the warehouse is closed. Factories that produced the pieces of machinery stored in the warehouse have closed down because there is no steel (the mills have closed) and the factories that used the finished pieces of machinery to produce wheels and pots and shoes and sewing machines are also closed. Only churches and schools seem to be open. Grocery stores, butcher shops, fish markets: All are closed, or have very little on their shelves. Just about every man on our block, on every block, is out of work. Ward and my father leave home every morning before dawn to look for jobs, but by noon, having found nothing, they come home.

By mid-December my father stops trying to find a job; he no longer goes out with Ward at dawn. Many mornings he does not even leave his bed. My mother presents potatoes, only potatoes, at every meal: boiled, baked, fried, in soup, as salad (when she can beg or borrow radishes or onions).

Ward leaves home for five days. He returns with

a bad cold. His hands and feet are almost frozen. "No jobs anywhere," he tells us. "Me and Teddy and Riley went all over Jersey and clear up into Mass. To Boston, Lynn, Springfield, everywhere. Everything's closed down, just like here. I fixed a guy's engine on his old Ford and he gave me thirty cents. He only had eighty-seven cents to begin with. I'll tell you something that's hard to believe. I saw people starving. Our own people right here in the United States of America—starving."

I hear outrage in his voice, and disappointment, and something else I've never heard in his or my father's voice. Fear.

My mother, still somewhat plump, still slightly rosy cheeked, still with melodies in her voice, sings her cheer. All this misery will pass very soon, she assures us, and she keeps on singing.

We wait. Everyone waits. But instead of factories opening, more close. Every day old friends leave the neighborhood. They just disappear.

I observe my father. The brave soldier has lost his battle. He is defeated. His body appears to have shortened. His shoulders stoop. Worry and fear have carved away muscle. His eyes, always bright, have dulled, swim deep inside dark sockets. Unable to feed his family, he is at first outraged, then sad, then humiliated.

It is the same with many mothers and fathers in too many homes up and down the street, all over Brooklyn, all over the United States.

Maybe if my father does not witness my hunger, he won't feel his failure. That's how he sees it: his failure. I make daily visits to the soup lines. The unemployed workers, almost all of them men, compose lines that reach around an entire block. There are, I hear, similar lines in other large cities.

At night I carry home to my mother and father chunks of bread dropped or stolen or bartered. My father knows. On his bed he stares at the wallpaper. He has hidden or perhaps thrown away the photograph of himself as a soldier.

Christmas Day Ward arrives with a large block of white cheese. We fall on it like the starving animals we have become. All except my mother, who continues to sit demurely, proudly, in a corner, unwilling, unable to eat. She stares through the window as if she's expecting Salvation to come galloping down the street and must be there to meet it.

All over the city, all over the United States, mothers are staring out of windows.

"Ward?"

"Yeah, Willy?"

"What was *The Crash*? Everyone talks about *The Crash*."

"Well, I'm not a professor, but there was the crash and then there was this depression."

"But what crashed?"

"The stock market crashed. I'm not sure, but I think that's a place here in New York where people go to gamble their own money and other people's money. One day last October the money everyone was gambling with wasn't worth more than a box of bubblegum wrappers. There wasn't enough gold to back up the paper and the coins. At least, that's the way I understand it. But you listen to five economists, you get six different explanations. All I know is, all over the country people who were millionaires in the morning were in the poorhouse that night. Banks shut down. There was no money. No money, no jobs. No jobs, no money. No jobs in Jersey, no jobs in Pennsylvania, no jobs in Ohio. Dad and me looked. We know."

1930. Ward seeks work all that spring, all that summer. Wherever he goes, he rides the freights. "They're fast and they don't cost anything." He does not call them "freights," he calls them "drags." Each time he returns home, his conversation is filled with more slang. Hobo slang.

"Willy, there's 'boes ridin' the rails all over the country. Kids young as eight or nine, old geezers in their nineties."

Ward is riding the drags somewhere west of Ohio when our mother dies. The once-cheerful woman had settled her body on the mattress and changed before my eyes. The way a caterpillar changes into a beautiful butterfly. This time the process was reversed. My mother's black hair turned gray in three days, her skin dried and shrank, her body curled in on itself, grew smaller and smaller. Every Sunday for years she has sung in the choir but now her strong voice breaks, grows weak, falls to a whisper, remains silent. My father hovers over her but she does not take notice. She dies at noon on July 4th.

"Your mother died of a broken heart," my father informs Ward when he eventually returns home. "A broken heart and an empty belly."

Every night I go to bed hungry. Every night I dream of my mother. In the dreams she offers me thick slabs of dark, sweet chocolate. I peel back the paper and thrust the candy into my mouth with such haste, with such force, I wake myself. Awake, I discover that my mouth and stomach are empty. Each night, after the persistent dream, I dig about in the pillow and among the blankets, but I never find a single chocolate bar.

"Keep your belly filled with water," Ward advises me. "That way, with your belly full, you won't think of food so much. I do it all the time, Willy."

In November, when Ward leaves home to look for work, I decide to go with him. Before he leaves, he sits with our father, who has been collecting cigarette butts all day in the neighborhood streets. I talk. My father empties the tobacco into a bowl. There is enough for five or six cigarettes. I try to convince my father that I am old enough to work.

"I might be able to find a job. You won't have to worry any longer, because I'll bring money home."

My father stops cutting the sports page into rectangles that will form his cigarettes. He stops measuring out the tobacco flakes. He appears surprised at my presence, at the sound of my voice. He is puzzled, as if the voices of both sons had been stilled long ago. Where have we come from?

Ward teaches me the fine art of catching and riding drags. After weeks of training sessions on dead freights—freights that have been shunted off on sidings and forgotten—and after hopping very slow drags, I ignore Ward's cautions and advance myself to more dangerous missions.

"The most important thing, Willy, is always go

for the front ladder. You miss the rear ladder, you can be dragged under the wheels. You grab the front and miss, all you'll do is you'll slide along the cinders. That can sort of smart. And be sure to pick a clear space to run in, so there won't be switches or signals to take off your arm. Or your head. You wait, you listen, you watch, you run alongside the car, you match its speed, then you dive for one of the rungs on the front ladder."

By late winter I am, at fifteen, a veteran. I see hundreds, thousands, of children like myself. Older and younger. Much younger. As young as eight or nine. They too run and dive for the ladders. Sometimes, at those slight inclines where the drag has not built up speed, hordes of hoboes, young and old, pour out of the woods to struggle aboard the cars. "Like rats runnin' to board a sinkin' ship," Ward says.

The children almost never travel alone, as the older hoboes do. Bundled in layers of clothing and almost as many layers of grime, they gather in groups of five or ten to protect one another. Their combined wills form the single weapon that defends them against destruction.

It is February 1931. We are in Weirton, West Virginia. We've not seen our father for more than a month. All day we've been repairing a basement for an old lady who has inherited four grandchildren whose parents are also scouting the country for jobs.

The woman has an unreliable old cow, eight tired Plymouth Rock hens, a Rhode Island Red rooster, and a large garden. She has hundreds of jars filled with vegetables and fruits, so the basement has to be dry and has to have strong shelves.

The woman has fed Ward and me, and instead of money, which she does not have, she gives us six jars of vegetables she canned the previous autumn.

"I want to see Dad," I say as I pound the last nail. "We have to take him this food."

"These jars? All the way to Brooklyn?"

"You don't think they'll make it?"

Ward starts to shake his head, but he stops and grins. He concedes the reversal of roles that has just begun.

"Well," he says, pointing to the stack of newspapers not yet shredded by rats, "the bottles will make it if we do. We'll wrap the jars with paper and rags and stuff them into a bundle we'll rope to our backs."

A few stars are visible, and a thin slice of moon. The air is almost too cold to breathe.

We walk along the tracks. Weirton is already a hundred miles to the south. Snow has not fallen for over a week, and what remains has been packed hard on the gravel, snapping like pistol shots under our feet.

Ward puts up his hand and stops. Trudging along with my head down, I almost run into him.

"I think I hear her." Ward crouches and feels the iron rails with his ungloved fingertips. He stands and pulls the glove back on. "A redball. She's ballin' the jack, Willy. Travelin' faster than fast."

The shivering earth sends tremors up through the snow, up through the holes in the soles of my shoes. Though the drag is still five or six minutes away, the muscles in my thighs begin to quiver.

"There she is," Ward says. "A double header."

Two engines shoot sparks and flame from their stacks, turning the immediate portion of night into a dull-orange glow.

"She's too fast for us, Willy."

I am too cold to wait all night for another drag. Even though my feet are wrapped with paper and my hands are double gloved, the thought of another hour without shelter or rest turns caution to desperation. I shift my shoulders to be sure my pack is secure.

"O.K.," Ward says. "You little mutt, if you can, I can. But me first."

I run close behind my brother. The noises of the iron wheels and the swaying steel cars are like continuous overlapping rolls of thunder. The cold iron walls brush my fingers. Never in the months I have been with Ward have I felt or seen or heard a drag move with such speed.

Running, I see Ward reach out and catch the rung of the front ladder of a car. The forward momentum swings him about with such force, I am sure I hear the thump of body against metal.

It is too late to check the run space ahead. I can only pray there are no signals ahead to tear my body.

As I run, I remove the ragged gloves and stuff them into the pockets of my long coat. The iron rungs will be cold, but cloth can slip. I flex my fingers to keep the blood flowing.

I appraise the speed and run as fast as my clothes and the pack will permit. In the dim moonlight I see the approaching car, the front ladder. I leap, catch a rung, hold on. The jerk, the swift toss of my body, the slam of my ribs against the metal force a scream up through my chest, but the padding of sweaters and jackets and coat saves me.

Hand over hand, grunting, I pull my body up until my feet find a rung. I rest a moment and then continue climbing until I am up and over the final rung. I stretch out on the deck, the flat walkway that spans the roof of the car, and I lie on my side to protect the jars.

When I sit up, my cold breath seems to clutch and freeze my heart. Outlined against the orange sky is the form of a man moving toward me, his silhouette grotesque against the orange light. I know I'm lost if it's a railroad cop, a bull. I can't run another inch, and my wrappings of cloth won't save me if I jump. I close my eyes and wait and hear laughter. When I open my eyes, I see Ward striding across the deck of the car ahead of mine, his cloth cap pushed back on his head. Ward is waving his arms and laughing as if finally aware he needn't worry about his baby brother anymore. It is the first time in weeks, in months, that I have heard my brother laugh.

We ride the drag into the Thirty-fourth Street station in Manhattan. Like most of the freights we've been riding, this one belongs to the Delaware, Lackawanna and Western Railroad.

II

Willy

1

In the spring—in March 1931—a tin shanty is erected on the bed of what once was the lower reservoir of Central Park. More shacks, all of tin, follow. The residents, as well as police officials (in their memos), call the village Hoover Valley, a salute to the President of the United States.

In late March my aunt loses the house in which Ward and my father and I have settled. Though her mortgage payments are small, my aunt has no money. She has no choice but to go to Delaware to live with her sister, who has no room for us. On the day before we are to leave the house—and with nowhere to go except a public flophouse, which is already filled with jobless men and hardworking bedbugs—Ward and my father and I visit Hoover Valley. My father seems to gain new energy at the sight of men and women building shelters, defying police, supporting each other, even, when possible, sharing food or tobacco or the primitive toilets and showers.

"You want to do it?" Ward asks.

My father nods. "I even know where my tools are. What's left of them."

By the end of April the park's green meadows are awash with flowers. The warm weather promises fair comfort to those who do not have even tin shanties to sleep in. Thousands of jobless, says *The New York Times*, are sleeping on benches or under trees or even in open meadows.

On the morning of the second Monday in May, my father leaves Hoover Valley to search for "a job of work," as he calls it. I never see him again.

"Gone to find a job," Ward says. "He'll be back."

The following Monday Ward does not return at dusk, as he always has, with a few coins or stale cookies or a sweater that still has sleeves.

"Gone to find a job," my friend Carl says. "He'll be back."

I know the truth. With employable adults in the

house, even if the house is a tin shanty and even if there is no employment to be found, Welfare can rule a family ineligible for full relief. Ward and my father, like many other men, have reasoned that as an orphan, the child left behind will at least be assured of the bread and the white margarine.

A week goes by and Carl gives up all efforts to reassure me. After all, Carl is here because he was orphaned more than a year before, when his father died.

On a Friday evening in late May, Deirdre, who has been sharing the neighboring shanty with her kid brother, Herbie, and their uncle, visits us in our shanty.

"We ought to all stay together," I say. "This place is bigger."

Herbie nudges Deirdre and whispers in her ear.

"We can't leave Norman," Deirdre says. "Norman moved in with us the other day. We—him and me—grew up together. He's Herbie's best friend."

"Thick glasses?" Carl asks.

"That's him." Deirdre laughs. "He jokes a lot."

"We need him," I say. "I can't remember the last time I laughed. What about your uncle?"

"What uncle? He's gone."

Two months after Ward left there are six kids living

together in the tin shack Ward and my father built in Hoover Valley.

"We have to go uptown. And maybe the Bronx." I try to explain ideas I've been thinking about all day. "This place is begged out. Too many standing around, waiting for handouts."

"What about the drags?" Carl asks. "You've told me all those stories about you and Ward. Why don't we get out of New York? Maybe to Jersey."

A unanimous "Yes!"

I take them, sometimes singly, sometimes in pairs, to the railroad yards. I recall Ward's advice and cautions, and pass on the advice, wishing Ward were here in my place.

They take to the rails as if born to them. Deirdre, smug about her talents, often defies me to match her feats. She would be even more daring if Herbie weren't there, trying to copy her leaps and grabs. Wherever she is, whatever she does, she never loses sight of Herbie, never surrenders her concern for his safety.

"We need a name," Deirdre says. "We're all together. We're like a family, and families have names."

"What ab-about Tom?" Norman says, giggling at the possibilities of the joke. Norman's stammer has only made him more appealing to us. We can rally around the defect. When someone outside tries to tease Norman, the gang, as one, can come to his defense.

Deirdre laughs and punches Norman's shoulder. "You ever hear of a family called Tom?"

"Well, I d-don't like Smith or J-Jones. There's a million Smiths and two m-million Joneses. How about Rockefeller? That's a g-good family n-name."

Herbie decides it. We're all in the Brooklyn railroad yards one August afternoon. Herbie points at a boxcar. "There."

"There what?" Deirdre says.

"That says Lackawanna, right?"

"Right. So my little brother can read. So?"

"Remember the gang of kids we met uptown? They were from Massachusetts. Remember?"

"So?"

"They were called Quincy."

"So?"

"So we ride the Lackawanna. It's an Indian name. Poppa told me once."

Deirdre nods. "It's a good name."

Norman adjusts his thick spectacles, removes them, cleans them with the flap of a greasy shirt. "I like T-Tom Rockefeller b-better."

* * *

Deirdre is fourteen. Her freckles are almost as red as her hair. She can outrun and outfight everyone except our new recruit, Slezak, who, at fifteen, has already earned money fighting in bars for men lucky enough to have nickels and dimes to spend on beer and gambling. Norman was the one who suggested we take Slezak in. "He's t-tough. Who knows when we'll need s-someone tough. I don't like to f-fight, but I sure l-like having s-someone around who c-can."

The first day Deirdre moved in, she announced she'd do her share of the cooking and cleaning, but only her share. No one disagreed. After all, Deirdre is a real benefit to Lackawanna. She can roll her eyes up into her head and stumble around so that even the Welfare nurses are convinced she's blind and has seizures. She and her little brother, in combination, can deliver double and triple the amount anyone else might bring to the pot at the end of each day.

Herbie is nine years old. He has a lisp that, a cop assured him, could charm the devil. He also has a boy-tenor voice that flows directly, according to his now-dead father, from the famous John McCormack. His repertoire includes seven Irish ballads and lullabies.

On the street, as they pick their way forward, Herbie's pale face is raised to the sky, and Deirdre, one hand on his shoulder, follows blindly, milk-white eyeballs surrounded by pale-red freckles. The rain of coins or fruit or sandwiches falls not into the tin cup, but into a tin bucket Deirdre carries in her long-fingered hands. The two of them, that perceptive and poetic cop adds, could milk coins out of the statues in the park.

Carl's family had lived in a single house like mine did, just down the block from ours, on Twenty-second Street. He and I used to work with tools from our basements, when we once had basements, and furnaces in those basements, and living rooms and bedrooms and kitchens above the basements, and families in those rooms. We share the role of carpenter now, expanding the tin shack, patching roofs, stacking the supporting boxes to serve as storage. While we poke about the city for boards and tin and discarded or overlooked tools, the others in Lackawanna are soliciting—meaning in most cases stealing—fruits and vegetables and candy and nuts and tobacco. Carl is the only one who smokes. "All for one and one for all," he reminds everyone. He is always reading *The Three Musketeers* and currently carries under his arm his fourth copy of the book, the other three having fallen apart. So, good musketeers, we never fail to collect butts for him.

Near the end of summer police and Parks Department officials express their concern about the growing number of shanties in Hoover Valley and the increasing sanitation problems. On the evening of September 21 Acting Captain George Burnell of Arsenal Station, supported by a squad of sympathetic but obedient patrolmen, forces everyone out of Hoover Valley. The shanties are razed, the land is bulldozed. Overnight the park is almost returned to its original state. Tin and lumber and rotten furniture are gone. In their place is dirt that will be grass next summer.

"Well, at least some people got work tearing it down and cleaning the park. But where," I ask the rest of Lackawanna, "do we go now?"

Carl has an idea. "There's this cellar room five blocks from here, where my dad used to bind books. He died. Binding books, he sure enjoyed that. I don't think anyone's been there since it was locked up. I bet it's just like it was when he left it. We could all stay there. And there's a furnace in the basement!" Carl leads the way down the street.

The house is deserted, as are several houses and even apartment buildings on either side. Boards have been nailed across the first-floor windows. After Slezak forces the hasp with an old screwdriver he's found near the steps, we enter the room very quietly, restraining our excitement. The rooms are large, with windows at street level. And orderly and clean.

We spend an hour stuffing one far corner with the equipment Carl's father used. Carl, the mechanical genius, promises to have the furnace working in a day or two.

Herbie is curious about the remnants of book-binding. He plays with the pages and pieces of leather and the presses. When he tries to get a response out of Carl, or tries to pull him to the corner where the material has been stored, Carl shakes his head and begs off, unwilling to see the stuff, to touch it, to revive memories.

"Leave him alone, Herbie," Deirdre calls. "Come help me dig up some sleeping things."

That's all that's needed to divert Herbie, a promise of a treasure hunt. They are quite successful. Mattresses and blankets are not too difficult to relay from local discard bins and from parked trucks recently packed by unfortunate and unwary neighbors. Coats and sweaters serve as blankets. Sacks of old clothes serve as pillows.

As promised, Carl has the furnace working the day after Lackawanna moves into the basement. This means we can use it on chilly evenings and, whenever we want to, for cooking. We have to have coal, especially for the cold nights coming on in a few weeks. We find pieces fallen from delivery trucks, pieces lifted from piles dumped at curbs and not yet transferred inside, pieces found in coal bins in old buildings now uninhabited. Lump by lump, pocket by pocket, bag by bag, until we have a good-sized mound at the side of the furnace. As the nights get colder, the basement continues warm and dry, so that no one, not even the perpetually cold Norman, wears more than underclothes to bed. Deirdre shares her mattress with Herbie. She always dresses and undresses under the coats she uses as blankets.

Carl attaches a long handle to an old baking pan so the pan can be placed in the furnace on the coals. On those days when a dead chicken or a piece of meat wanders into a pocket, there are hot meals.

The ever-versatile and delicious potato is a rare and sorely missed treat. But Slezak staggers into the basement one afternoon, a crate of potatoes on his shoulder. He has carried the crate twelve blocks. "They fell off a truck. Six crates. The truck kept on going. I grabbed one of the crates that wasn't broke. Filled it back up and ran. People came out of doors and windows with buckets and pans and sacks. In maybe five minutes there wasn't a potato in the snow. Look. Big potatoes."

Morning, noon, night, and in between, someone is sitting in the room or walking the street munching a black-skinned steaming potato as if it's an apple.

"Only th-thing I like b-better is ch-chocolate c-cake."

"But you can't live on chocolate cake," Herbie says. "Even I know that."

"How ab-ab-about chocolate cake and baked p-potatoes?"

No longer having to talk about the heat or the cold, we talk about food.

Deirdre: Sardines and rye bread. I know that's not Irish, but sardines are my favorite. The ones in oil. I'll give a hug to anyone gets me one of those sort of round cans with sardines in tomato sauce.

Herbie: Oh boy, peanut butter. With crackers. Or bread. Or dig in with a knife. Or your finger. This finger next to your thumb. Scoop it out around the edge with your finger. Oh boy, oh boy.

Willy: Bologna sandwiches. Any kind of bread, but that Jewish black rye's the best. With mustard and catsup and mayonnaise and pickles. Those big fat ones from the Lower East Side, the ones in barrels. Breakfast, dinner, supper, seven days a week, I'll take bologna sandwiches over chicken.

Norman: Anything, everything, b-but there's g-gotta b-be chocolate cake in th-there s-somewhere. B-b-before, after, in the m-middle. And root b-beer. Phooey on milk. I'll take root b-beer.

Carl: We can't ever have my favorite. Bratwurst. My mother made it better than anyone. All my aunts and uncles paid her to make bratwurst. My father said he'd fight off wolves to have my mother's bratwurst. I'll never be able to eat anyone else's, no matter what.

Slezak: Steak every meal. A fighter at McCarthy's says it's meat gives you strength. Every match, four hours before he went in the ring, he ate steak. So I'll take hamburger until I can afford steak. Someday, you wait. Steak for every meal. Almost raw.

Norman: Yeah, hamburger. With a th-thick slice of onion.

Deirdre: And slices of tomatoes.

Norman:	And ch-chocolate cake.
Slezak:	Cake softens your muscles.
Norman:	I like s-soft m-muscles.
Deirdre:	And ruins your eyes.
Norman:	You c-can always b-buy glasses.
Slezak:	Steak. With baked potatoes.
Norman:	O.K. B-baked potatoes. And steak, c-coated with ch-chocolate.

It is Deirdre's suggestion. Thanksgiving has to be celebrated. "My favorite holiday, next to Christmas. How about this, Willy? There are six of us. We break up into three groups, two in each. We go to missions or churches or whatever. We eat what they give us and get whatever extra we can. Seconds, things left in pans, maybe even trade off things for food. Then, at night, we'll have another supper. Our own. We'll warm up everything—"

"Not the ch-chocolate c-cake."

"Norman, we're gonna *boil* your chocolate cake."

"But we ought to go to more than just one church," I tell them. "Everyone celebrates in different ways."

"Yeah," Slezak agrees. "I like different kinds of food. You ever taste Ukranian? They make something at Easter—"

"But this isn't Easter, Sleze." Carl laughs.

*   *   *

We're gone all day. Deirdre takes Herbie, of course. Norman and I go together, and Carl joins Slezak. We are back by seven o'clock, and by eight are well into our second Thanksgiving dinner.

There is turkey (from a Catholic charity, remains packed in little white boxes packed in turn in brown paper bags), vegetables from a Jewish charity (Jews, Lackawanna decides, have more fresh fruits and vegetables than Catholics or Protestants), desserts from a Protestant mission (no one bakes better cookies or cakes than little gray-haired grandmothers in Baptist or Presbyterian churches, though Episcopalians, Carl swears, produce the finest pumpkin pies—which, however, after transportation from borough to borough, in pockets and bags, might as well have been stewed by aborigines).

Stuffed, half asleep, staring dumbly at the empty plates, everyone grumbles when I mention the word "money." They're barely awake enough to respond.

As usual Deirdre and Herbie have earned the most, $2.56, almost twice as much as all others combined. Norman and Carl are almost even, having panned forty cents and forty-one. I've returned with thirty-eight cents, only thirteen of which, I admit, I've panned. I found a quarter on the steps of a church.

"I thought about it for maybe an hour. Should I keep it or give it to the preacher? Norman convinced me."

"I s-said it was b-better to give than re-receive, and the church gave it so he ought to re-re-receive it."

Slezak, who feels that begging money somehow indicates inferiority, refuses to beg from anyone but men who look as if they might challenge him to a fight. He puts fourteen cents into the box.

Norman controls the money box, not because he is more disciplined or more capable at arithmetic, but because his father worked in a bank. He must, therefore, have talent.

"Hey! Big news! We got seven dollars and fifty-three cents in the box. We're rich! We c-c-c-can buy two hundred ch-chocolate c-cakes."

It is after midnight. Warm and drowsy, we talk softly about our good fortune. Is this a sign? Will it continue?

"Good luck doesn't have anything to do with it," I say.

Slezak disagrees. "What about all those guys out there in the doorways? All curled up and freezin'? What about them? Are they lucky? They're *un*-lucky!"

Norman shivers. "D-don't t-talk about c-cold."

Deirdre reaches over to pull a blanket closer around Herbie, who is trying to keep his eyes open. "They haven't gotten together," she says. "If they got together with five or six others, like we did, they could be warm and stuffed too."

Carl is impressed. "With seven fifty-three in the bank. That's how much my dad brought home every *week*."

We wait, but Carl offers nothing more. No one speaks very often about home, about why we're scrounging on the streets, but when someone, almost by mistake, does open up, it's brief, a comment offered and quickly deserted.

Herbie's thin voice pipes up, surprising everyone. He was nodding just moments ago. "I can't remember being so—well—just glad." He slides closer to Deirdre, who punches his pillow to prepare a depression to receive his head. She places an arm around his shoulder and hugs him against her body.

"We b-better stay to-together," Norman says, wiping his thick eyeglasses. "Last Thanksgiving I had c-crackers for supper and they were st-stale. I st-stood in line at a place, and by the t-time I g-got to the women at the c-counter, all the food was gone. Except c-crackers. They were st-stale."

Slezak does not give up. "I still say it's luck. We got together at Hoover Valley. What if we hadn't gone there? What if we were in some small town where there aren't many kids to get together? We'd be alone, tryin' to make it alone."

"Like some of those k-kids you see on the st-streets. I k-kinda ag-agree with S-Sleze."

"Yeah," Deirdre says. "But what about those gangs of kids like Quincy? The Scranton Boomers. And that gang at Coney Island last summer. There were about twenty kids."

"The Loop," I say. "That's a place in Chicago. One of the kids told me. They all lived right around the el. So they called their gang The Loop."

"They were one big family," Deirdre says, almost sadly, as if the word triggers memories.

"All for one and one for all," Carl chants. "If there were only three of us, we could be The Three Musketeers."

"Well, we c-could c-call ourselves The Six Musketeers."

I strike the floor with the palm of my hand. "We *have* a name. We're *Lackawanna*."

Carl laughs. "Hey, when I get old and get married and my wife takes my name and we have kids . . ."

We all laugh and contribute possible names. Bobby Lackawanna . . . Lucy Lackawanna . . . Betty and Herman Lackawanna . . .

Herbie sits up and cheers. "There'll be little Lackawannas all over the country." He looks up into Deirdre's face. "Deirdey, let's sing Mom's favorite song. She always—"

Deirdre hugs him and finishes his sentence. "She always sang it at Thanksgiving."

They sing in misty-eyed duet. It is a song about Ireland's green hills. Deirdre, alone, sings a song her father composed. There are references to moons shining on lakes and swans floating in silvery moonlight and red roses tossed on waves by star-crossed lovers. Deirdre murmurs, after her song trails off like the whisper of a ghost, that the song was written by Herbert Callahan.

Slezak follows, with songs his mother used to recite in Czech. She was too embarrassed to try to sing them. Every Thanksgiving she would sit at the head of the table, reminding everyone how fine a man their father had been and how strong.

"After two cars crush him between them when he's clean the street," Slezak says, imitating his mother's broken accent and her proud full-chested bearing, "your father, he walk home with both legs broke."

Norman, whose family never celebrated any holiday, Jewish or Christian, except Thanksgiving, tells a story he makes up on the spot. It is a combination of what might pass for truthful fiction, the theme and the plot somewhat secondhand, containing elements of O. Henry's "The Gift of the Magi" deftly transferred to Thanksgiving.

"Last year," Carl says, since it is his turn, "my family joined two other families. It was Thanksgiving, but we had soup. Only soup. But what a soup! This other man, from the other family, he closed down his butcher shop. He brought home his last four chickens and fifty-six extra chicken feet. Everyone put their flour together and there was enough for eight loaves of bread and four pumpkin pies and—get this, Norman—a big chocolate cake."

The silence that follows the last reminiscence contains a strange melancholy. As if the whispers and songs and memories have formed a solid bulk of another person that fills the room.

We're doing O.K. We're eating, we have hot water for baths and we even wash our clothes sometimes. The furnace goes all the time now, and someone is always bringing in coal.

One afternoon—it is Tuesday, December 15th—Deirdre and Carl burst into the cellar. Deirdre, always cool and composed no matter what the crisis, is hysterical. When Slezak and Norman and I try and fail to calm her, Carl has to tell the story.

"Herbie was kidnaped." He gulps and digs at an eye with his fist. "He kidnaped Herbie."

2

"Do something! Do something, Willy!"

Her freckles seem to pop out on her white skin as Deirdre screams. I hold her and finally calm her enough so Carl can tell us what happened.

"Me and Deirdre and Herbie were in the Thirty-fourth Street yards. There was a milk train came in from upstate New York. Cans were being cleaned for the trip back upstate. Across the tracks was a line of flatcars loaded with Christmas trees. You could smell them. Herbie said it smelled like home at Christmas, and he was going over to see maybe he could find a branch to bring back."

Deirdre, in her weeping, cries, "Herbie, Herbie."

"Deirdre finds this refrigerator car. Some 'boes had already broken the seal. The car was raided long before we got there, that was plain. Vats of butter and broken eggs and boxes of cheese everywhere. And carcasses of chicken. The weather's so cold, almost nothing has melted. Me and Deirdre got some sticks and rocks and broke through the ice. We filled our pockets and our jackets. We could hardly walk, we had so much, and we started to go. Deidre called Herbie. He was over by the flatcars, talking to this big 'bo. There was something about him. I knew he couldn't be a bull. Never saw a bull wear an overcoat too small for him. Or a fur cap with flaps over the ears, tied under his chin. He was a 'bo."

Deirdre shakes herself free of my arms. "Let's go! Let's go after him. We're just standing here!"

"We have to know what happened, Deirdre. We'll be worse off if we just run around yelling." I catch her in my arms again. She stops pleading, but she does not stop weeping.

"Herbie turned when Deirdre called, and started walking toward us. Right then a line of empties starts moving out of the yard. There were cars from different roads, different places, but most were from three lines: the Chicago Junction, the Indiana Harbor Belt, the Chicago River and Indiana."

"Good. That might help."

"Herbie takes maybe three or four steps toward us when this 'bo—he was big, about the biggest man I've ever seen—he calls Herbie's name. Herbie looks back, says something, and keeps walking toward us. We can see the big 'bo running after him, but Herbie can't see him. We just stand there."

Slezak pounds one fist into the other. "I'll get him. I don't care how big he is. Come on!"

I hold up my hand to Slezak. "Wait a few minutes. We have to be calm."

"Calm!" Deirdre yells. "Calm? He's taken Herbie!"

"The big 'bo catches Herbie and carries him back to the freight and throws him in an open car. Herbie leaps out, and the big 'bo catches him and throws him back in. Then *he* jumps in, keeping Herbie from jumpin' out. He slides the door closed. You know it takes almost all of us to close one of those doors? He closes it with one arm."

Deirdre, almost cried out, is moaning. She crumples to the floor, onto her mattress.

"By the time we reach the tracks, the crummy's fifty yards away. We run until we can't run anymore. The caboose, I mean the crummy, it's disappeared."

After a long, dreary silence, broken only by Deirdre's moans and hoarse breaths, Carl finishes the story.

"We threw away the chickens and the cheese. We found two bulls, but they didn't care. When we told them what happened, they just walked away. Deirdre grabbed one of them, begged him for help. He just shook her off. Waved an ax handle at her. Said we were lucky we were kids, or we'd have lumps on our heads by now. He chased us out of the yards. That's it."

It is after six o'clock. Lackawanna is in the cellar. No use going to the city bulls, I know. "They're like that railroad bull. One more lost kid. So? So add him to the other hundred or thousand."

"Yeah. K-kids disap-disappear every day. All over the c-country. G-good riddance."

Deirdre sits up. "Willy, I'm not just sitting here."

"We'll do it ourselves. We'll track them down." But as I talk, I know the difficulties. "It's gonna be tough. None of you has been farther away than Jersey. We can get around O.K. here, in the city, but we might have to go farther. Well, let's do it. We're together. We have to stay together. If we do, we'll get Herbie back."

"That 'b-bo c-could have Herbie out of the s-state by now, W-Willy."

Deirdre groans.

Slezak, raising both fists, begs God to let him be there when we find the 'bo.

"Deirdre, do you know what time it was when he grabbed Herbie?"

Deirdre shakes her head, refuses—or is unable—to think, to remember. Carl answers for her. "About four. I remember when we found the first bull. He had his watch out, winding it. It was ten after four."

"O.K., it's not dark yet. So it's around six. What direction was the drag going?"

"South. Right, Deirdre?"

She nods, but seems unable to use her voice.

"It was a string of empties, fruit and vegetable cars mainly. Most were from the Chicago River and Indiana."

"Chicago's near Indiana. Right?" Slezak asks.

"Right. N-near Chi-Chicago."

"I've got a plan. Carl and Slezak should check out the banana train that runs from Weehawken and connects with the West Shore line. That will get them onto the ferries from the Seventy-second Street station. They should talk to anyone who might be useful. Deirdre and Norman and me are going back to Thirty-fourth."

We're all ready to go except Deirdre. She's kneeling in the corner, praying.

Since we've been together, none of us has gone to church except for handouts. At one time or another each of us has accepted pieces of clothing and occasionally a bed without feeling it necessary to admit or promise gratitude. Now, as Deirdre prays, I, like the rest, hesitate. Should I act as if nothing special is happening? But something special *is* happening. I can tell everyone else feels the same.

As the accepted leader, I can't ignore Deirdre. Even if I wanted to, I can't pretend I'm unmoved. For a moment I consider the possibility of getting down on my own knees, of joining her in prayer. It can't hurt, it might help.

I have a flash of recall. There's my mother, standing with such pride among the other members of the choir. Her clear voice rises like a bird's above the group. Her eyes shine, their joy visible from the last row in the church. My father, even though he never entered the church, always indulged her. Not just indulged—he admired her, always walked her to evening prayer meetings.

I turn my head to locate the sound of murmured words. It is Norman. His eyes are closed behind the thick lenses, and his lips form words in a strange language. Carl, at Norman's side, watches me. Is he remembering? Yes.

We—Carl and I—had lived on the same block,

had begun first grade the same day, had been together through eighth grade. Each of us had eaten and slept at the other's home. Our families had suffered the same shocks in almost the same sequence: peace, security, sudden loss of jobs, fear, hunger, death, breakup. When we met in Hoover Valley, Carl was alone. By now each of us knows the other's story, each of us can recall the features of the other's mother or father.

What is Carl remembering now? The night my mother taught him—he was eight years old then—the Lord's Prayer and Carl rushed upstairs to report to his own mother that his father was known, in Heaven, as Art?

Deirdre rises, crossing herself. Carl, as if he's been waiting for this moment, quickly opens the door and leads the rest of us out.

Carl and Slezak pull their caps down over their ears and move away, into the darkness. Deirdre starts across the street.

"Come on, we have to catch them now."

She stops in the middle of the street and pauses, alone, then she returns. Gazing into my face, she all but admits defeat. The old buoyancy that had carried her day after day since she and Herbie began wandering the streets is missing.

"C'mon," I say. "We'll find him."

Norman's teeth are chattering. He wraps a scarf around his throat. It covers his face to his eyes. "You b-bet we will."

Deirdre, almost jogging, leads the way. When she slows and turns, her face betrays her fatigue. "Every night, ever since we left home, he goes to sleep holding my hand."

3

By the time we reach the Thirty-fourth Street station, three hours have passed since the big 'bo kidnaped Herbie. I lead the way over rails, under and over gates and fences, around engines puffing and steaming like huge beasts preparing to charge. The night lights in the yards are bright. With Deirdre and Norman behind me, I dart from shadow to shadow to evade brakies, conductors, baggage men, track crews.

"You stay here," I tell Deirdre and the shivering Norman. "I'll go ahead and see what's up. It's easier for one to move around here than three." Deirdre finds an alcove in the wall of a shed, and she huddles there with Norman close against her.

I approach a worker who is checking the waste traps of the only assembled freight in sight, a line of ten or fifteen coal cars, all of them empty.

Trying to appear smaller and younger than I am, weakening my voice, affecting an impressive limp, I manage to approach within a few feet of the man. The worker hears my footsteps and looks up. Recognizing the figure before him to be that of a child, the man laughs, as if he appreciates the joke the darkness played on him.

"Sir, I need help. I lost my little brother."

"Well, I ain't found him. What in blue blazes are you and your little brother doin' out here at night, anyway? Why ain't you home? Ah, don't answer that question."

"It was about four o'clock, sir. Did you see him? He's smaller than me. He's nine years old."

"You really got a little brother? Cripes, you ain't knee high to a grasshopper yourself. How old is he?"

"Nine, sir. Sort of pale, and he has freckles and he's wearing, well, he's wearing clothes like mine."

"He got as many rags on as you got, he'll be warm at least. You kids, runnin' loose like jackrabbits. There's two or three of you behind every pole, waitin' to hop anything got wheels on it." His voice, irritated at first, has grown friendly, almost fatherly. "You kids cross the country these days like you're goin' 'cross Broadway."

"Yessir, I agree."

"You're the first one I met has good manners." The worker has a cigar in his mouth. The end, clenched between his teeth, has probably been chewed on since the previous payday. As he gazes down at me, the cigar, manipulated by his tongue, rolls from one corner of his mouth to the other. "You serious, youngster?"

"Yessir. Honest. I was standing over there, where that engine's steaming. Number 406. Near those flats with the Christmas trees. A drag . . . a freight was going out. I looked up. A big 'bo, the biggest man I ever saw, was walking toward Herbie. He grabbed my little brother and threw him in a boxcar and jumped in after him. I ran but couldn't catch it."

"He's how old?"

"Nine, sir."

"I'll tell you. I ever catch a hobo with a young boy, he better give his soul to God, because he's givin' his head to me. You come along. How'd you hurt your leg? The freights?"

"Yessir."

I follow the man across the yard, careful not to trip before the moving cars, to be alert for switches, to say yessir at every admonition to watch my step. Twice I forget to limp, but I catch myself before the man looks back.

We approach the building I know to be the roundhouse, a combination of steel struts and beams and arches and high many-paned windows that couldn't have been cleaned since the Civil War. Engines, and occasionally cars, are brought here for cleaning and repairs. A sleek black one-eyed animal is at rest, panting, on one of the many pairs of rails that cross the turntable. After work is completed, the turntable and the engine, steel and brass polished to a high gloss, will pivot so the huge wheels can move it into the yard, where other engines wait their turn to be bathed and polished.

In the pit underneath the engine, grease-smeared men are working acetylene torches. Coveralled men on the surface drift in and out of steam clouds. I cover my ears to protect them from the slamming of metal on metal, the blasts of steam, the shrill whistles. I clamp my teeth against the taste of grease and soot.

The worker leads me to the end of the roundhouse, past a section of bins containing parts of wheels and rods and gears. He calls, telling me to follow. I do, up a series of steps and into a room where a man sits in front of an immense map of the United States, cobwebbed with colored lines, each line representing a major or minor railroad.

The man sitting before the map has a green-shaded cap low over his eyes. His black vest hangs loosely on his bony frame. The sleeves of his white shirt are rolled up to the elbows. He and his desk, which is covered with papers, are contained within the cone of light sent down by the green-shaded bulb hanging from the ceiling.

"Describe your little brother and the 'bo that grabbed him," the worker tells me.

I rely on Deirdre and Carl's description of the 'bo but again describe Herbie as I did a few minutes before.

"What time you say he was grabbed?"

"Close to four. The drag . . . the freight was headed south."

"That don't mean too much in a yard," the man in the vest says. "A train headin' south one minute can be headin' north five minutes later. That's why we got switches."

"Well, it had about thirty cars. Most of them from Chicago Junction, Indiana Harbor Belt, and Chicago River and Indiana."

"Now that's info I can use."

The man pulls the green eyeshade lower over his

nose and begins shuffling papers, checking schedules, leafing through notebooks, fingering a detailed map of New York City. He removes a gold watch from a pocket in his black vest and considers its face. He mutters to himself, lists and adds and subtracts numbers on several sheets of paper and then, nodding his head as if agreeing with previous theories, he lifts the earpiece of the telephone from its cradle. "Stevenson, Thirty-fourth Street station, New York Central."

After an exchange of a few quips and three short hiccup-laughs, Stevenson relays the descriptions I have given him.

"Yeah, looks like a big jocker. Well, if he's stolen this boy away, he's a jocker, ain't he? Why else'd he kidnap a boy? Yeah, thanks. Yeah, spread the word. You get any info, you can call me here." He excuses himself, turns the phone from his face, and asks me where I can be reached.

I shuffle my feet, shake my head.

"I don't have a phone. But there's one near the post office near where I live. Can I call you later, from there? How soon? If we wait too long—"

"Goin' right off and goin' in the wrong direction is worse than waitin' and goin' in the right direction." He brings the phone to his mouth again. "Get the info to me, I'll get it to the boy at this end." He listens for a short time, thanks the person at the other end and hangs up.

The worker who led me here points a finger at the man in the green eyeshade. "This is Stevenson. He's a dispatcher, a librarian, a detective, you name it. What's your name, son?"

"Willy. It's really William."

"William, meet Mr. Stevenson. Stevenson, meet really William."

"Can't I call you in a while?" I ask again.

"Well, it's gettin' complicated. Here I am coverin' for a man who's sick. I should have been out of here an hour ago. O.K., O.K., I'll tell you what. Call me here in five or six hours. That'll give us time to track everything down. If it takes more than six hours, I'll give you Mac's number in Buffalo, the man I just talked to."

"Buffalo? What's he know?"

Stevenson, with a sigh, leans back in his swivel chair. "Buffalo," he says, "is the center of New York Central's Car Service Department. Hundreds of people doin' nothin' but keepin' records on each and every freight train. Not just the NYC, but other trains too. Even foreign cars. Once a car's spotted on a siding, set off in a yard, or put out along the line, conductors report the location and its consist. Its contents. Buffalo can say in ten or fifteen minutes what train's goin' where and where it is this minute and if a car's where it should be or shouldn't be."

"But how can they help Herbie? And if it only takes ten or fifteen minutes, why wait for five—?"

"The word's goin' out. Telegraphers all around the area are tappin' it out across the wire. Five hundred pairs of eyes'll be scoutin' the rails, watchin' for the least little sign of that big 'bo or that boy."

Stevenson then writes three phone numbers on a piece of paper and identifies each one. "This is my number here. This is my number at home. This is Mac in Buffalo. Now don't lose it."

"I sure won't."

"I wrote down my schedule, too."

The man in coveralls thanks Stevenson and nudges me to the door and out of the office.

"You're gonna call Stevenson in five-six hours. You got a nickel?"

"Sure I do. Thanks, anyway."

The worker grins. "Oh, I wasn't gonna give you a nickel. All I asked was do you have one. Well, I gotta get to work."

He walks toward the freight he was checking when I first approached him. He waves his arm. "You take care of yourself, youngster. And don't forget to call Stevenson. He's a gentleman."

I wave back, call, "Thanks," and return to the shed where Deirdre and Norman are stamping their feet and flapping their arms.

"Norman's freezing," Deirdre says. "What do we do? What'd you find out?"

As cold as she is, she is obviously ready to go on from here, to stay out in the cold all night if necessary.

"Aw, I'm not c-cold. Ch-chattering my t-teeth k-keeps me warm. It's ex-exercise."

"Come on, Willy, what happened? Did you hear any news?"

I tell her everything. She requires the most minute details, but in the end is disappointed.

" '*Wait*,' he says. "O.K., O.K. I'll wait. Maybe he's right, maybe you're right. But if they're hundreds of miles away, we might never catch them. Herbie could be gone forever."

Back at the basement, Deirdre rushes in first, calling, "Herbie? Are you here, Herbie?"

Carl and Slezak are sitting on their mattresses, their backs against the wall. They are drinking strong-smelling coffee. They appear sullen, defeated. Slezak shakes his head in reply to Deirdre's unasked question.

"We talked to maybe fifty people," Carl tells her. "We didn't find anyone who's seen a big 'bo with a boy. You find anything?"

I tell all the main points again, now and then conceding to Norman's stammered contributions. Having removed his two coats and three sweaters and his scarf, Norman is backed up against the furnace, absorbing heat through the layers of clothing that remain. He sips the steaming coffee from the chipped blue mug.

Deirdre has collapsed on her mattress, her hand going out to locate the spot where Herbie's head has so often rested.

Slezak, furious, throws himself into his push-ups. He normally performs his rigid ritual of bodybuilding in the early morning, but now, spitting out oaths, he promises vengeance when we catch the 'bo. He has no doubts that we'll succeed, eventually. When we do, he'll be ready.

For the first time I'm angry—I almost yell at Slezak. Under the quaint manners, his old-country courtesy, Slezak is famous for his temper and is often avoided because of it. Anger isn't what's needed now, I think. We have to be calm and patient. But I also resent Slezak's assumption of lawmaker and justice giver. Lackawanna, Deirdre said, is a family. One person can't make the decisions for all. As leader, I can lead, but I can't dictate. I don't want to and they wouldn't let me.

In my travels with Ward, I witnessed violence. Too much of it. Ward tried to shield me from it, protected me when it approached too closely to us, but I've seen drunken hoboes in boxcars slashing each other with knives, beating each other with clubs. I've seen men, and on occasion women, suddenly change into animals over as trivial an event as a borrowed cigarette or an imagined unfair distribution of soup. I've seen railroad bulls, intent on keeping their jobs, so strongly identify with the railroad owners that even the simplest act of abuse against a freight car was taken as a personal offense. They almost used their clubs with glee. Only Ward's size and strength and his intuition—where was the danger? when was it due? who was offering it?—served him and me on occasions I try now not to remember.

Neither Ward nor my father, and certainly not my mother, had ever committed a brutal act. But is brutality, in its time, essential? Isn't the life I am living brutal? Aren't Ward and my father, and I, and everyone in this room, everyone in all such rooms—aren't we all too placid? Too accepting? Shouldn't we be filled with anger, as Slezak is? Shouldn't we yearn to strike back, as Slezak yearns?

"We just have to wait, Sleze. We'll call Stevenson and then decide what to do."

"In five hours," Deirdre wails, "it'll be nine hours since he was grabbed. They'll be so far away. Oh, Herbie . . ."

Norman and Carl sit beside Deirdre, one taking her hand, another offering her coffee. Slezak, in deference to her, stops his oaths and his exercises. He sits and stares; then he too tries, to no avail, to convince Deirdre that a cup of coffee will make her feel better.

Among hundreds of items in our junk box there was once an alarm clock. I recall seeing it there. I find the box, withdraw hammers and chisels and screwdrivers and pliers and nails and screws and hooks and balls of string and wrenches and fragments of motors and shoelaces and belts and buckles and keys and can openers and knives, and under a coil of rope two clocks, one of which promises to function. I wind it, set the alarm, test it. The alarm rings. I reset the alarm, giving myself five hours to sleep.

Deirdre is quiet, but I know she is staring up at the ceiling. I reach out to pat the mound that has to be her feet. Deirdre, sniffling, turns onto her side, facing away from me, but she keeps hold of my hand.

While untying my shoes, before crawling under

the blankets, I think of my father. Lying in the darkness, I think of him again. The voice comes soon after the face appears. My father told me several times that it's easier to get your feet warm if you remove your shoes.

"If your feet are warm, your whole body's warm. Unless your head's bald. Then you better wear a cap. Cover your head, uncover your feet. Something to remember, William. A little bit of information you'll never have to use."

I try to ignore Deirdre's sobs. I try to force my memories into oblivion. But my father's face remains.

Poppa, you never expected your advice would be useful. But look, I'm warm. I've told everyone, and they're warm. We're lucky, Poppa, we all have lots of hair on our heads. Norman's the only one who wears caps. He has more hair than any of us but his head's always cold. I told Norman what you said, Poppa. I tell them things—what you used to say, what Ward taught me—I tell them all the time.

4

The five bundles of cloth stir when the alarm rings. Unable, in the darkness, to find the switch to turn off the alarm, I stuff the clock down among the coats and blankets.

The others are awake, putting on their clothes, but I insist they go back to sleep. "I'll make the call and be right back."

After I draw on my socks and wrap both feet with newspaper, my toes and heels do not slide around inside my shoes. They are fine shoes, almost new, but they are at least one size too large. I bought them a week ago, knowing I'd be wrapping my feet all winter. By summer I'll need new shoes, and then I can search out a pair that will fit without the insulation.

As I open the door, I feel someone prodding my back. It is Deirdre. She has bundled up for the walk to the post office.

"You forgot something," she says as we leave the basement. She holds out her hand. "You can't use the telephone for free." She jingles some coins.

Holding the paper Stevenson gave me, tilting it to see the numbers clearly in the light cast by the single globe on the pole ten or fifteen feet away, I lose a nickel because I dial incorrectly.

"No, this ain't Stevenson!" And the man, aroused from his sleep, slams down the receiver in whatever room he's fortunate enough to be in.

As Deirdre, standing ten feet away in better light, reads and calls out the numbers, I dial slowly. On the fifth ring, a sleepy voice says, "Stevenson."

"This is Willy. I talked to you tonight about—"

"I been sitting here waiting. If you didn't call, I was gonna go looking for you personally to wring your neck. I oughta be home getting my beauty sleep."

"Thanks for staying, sir."

"O.K. Reason I stayed is I got some info."

"You did?" I shout with such joy that Deirdre

crowds close to me, forcing her head near the receiver so she can hear, too. "Did you find Herbie?"

"Hold your horses, there, just hold your horses. The train that big 'bo caught was out of Thirty-fourth all right. Engine number 406. It left Thirty-fourth at four oh four. The 'bo and your little brother were seen on it. They were still on it in Harrisburg, where one of our detectives threw them off. The boy tried to talk to the detective, but the 'bo whisked him away. Ain't too unusual these days. Quite a few older hoboes got themselves a young slave and live high, the devils."

I try to shift my body so Deirdre won't hear Stevenson's news. If her fears aren't verified, she might be able to pretend they aren't there. But she tugs at my arm, drawing the receiver close to her ear too.

"Our detective chased them down the tracks. The big 'bo held the boy's hand, dragging him. Two hours later, when engine 406 pulled out of Harrisburg, the two of them must have got back on. They were on it when it arrived in Altoona. Another detective tells me there's a hobo jungle there. The 'bo and your little brother probably needed food. They'll get it there. That's it. That's all the info I have right now."

"We're . . . I'm going there. To Altoona."

"You'll get there too late, you know. Twelve, maybe

fourteen hours too late. This weather's causing all kinds of trouble with schedules."

"We have to do it."

"Now listen, young 'un. You're a boy with good manners. Courteous. And you've got spunk. I'd like to get your little brother outa that devil's hands. You call me every so often at this number. Maybe I can get more info for you. Remember, I don't regularly work this shift. I told you what my regular schedule is. I wrote it down. You keep that slip. Don't you go and lose it. I've got a question."

"O.K."

"Why haven't you gone to the police? This is a crime. The man has to be punished."

"Mr. Stevenson, you don't understand. There are hoboes everywhere. And kids—runaways, orphans, all kinds. The cops can't do anything, even if they want to. By the time they'd get around to it, it'll be too late. We . . . I . . . have to get Herbie away from him as soon as we can."

"O.K., O.K., you're the boss. You're out there. I ain't, thank God. He's your brother, not mine. You take care, young 'un. I'm going home and get my beauty sleep."

"Thanks, Mr. Stevenson." But Stevenson has already hung up.

Deirdre cannot trust what she thinks she's heard. She wants every word repeated, but I'm selective. As I tell her what she's already heard once, she keeps nodding. Then, after I'm finished, she puts her mittened hand to my cheek.

"You said he was your little brother."

"Well, he is, sort of."

In an effort to minimize attention all of Lackawanna, all five of us, board the Pennsylvania at different points along the route, early in the morning. I am first to grab a car, at seven o'clock sharp. Slezak is fifth, at seven twelve. After locating each other, we settle down in a Pennsylvania & Ohio boxcar near the end of the line. My body is trembling as the freight rolls along, and I smile to myself as Ward's voice comes to me: "Empties ride hard, Willy. The car can have a flat wheel, or the springs can be shot. Tensions in a boxcar's springs are designed for heavy loads, so an empty car bounces more than a loaded one. If there's only empties, try and catch one between two loaded cars. That cuts down the empty's bouncin'."

The car Slezak found has no flat wheels and, fortunately, has a filled and sealed car at either end. Huddled together for warmth in a corner of the car, with the heavy door pulled closed to shut out the wind and snow, Lackawanna is soon a mass of bodies that do not stir at the various stops, nor at the shiftings where a car or two is expelled onto sidings. Any 'bo happening to crawl into the car would probably mistake the bodies for sacks of meal dumped aboard by a careless baggage master. I know, however, there is little likelihood many 'boes will be riding the line in this weather. Most will be hunkered down in cities, close to a mission. Or already in California.

I am the first to awaken. I decide it must be close to noon because the door, open an inch or two, displays a light suggesting late morning or early afternoon. I'm hungry. Somewhere, inside one or another of my sweaters, shirts, and jackets, is a chunk of a candy bar, but if I dig it out I'll disturb Deirdre, who has settled against my right side. Carl is slumped against my left, and Norman has draped his long lean body across Carl's knees. Slezak, who is forever insisting he is filled not with blood but with antifreeze, lies alone, curled on himself. Clouds of frosted breath come out of the separate clumps of cloth.

If I could free my arms, I could rub my eyes and, as well, dig around for that candy bar. One arm would do it, the arm on Carl's side. The movement lifts Carl, who promptly drops back into place, his heavy breathing undisturbed. I rub both eyes, yawn, rub again, and permit myself one small bite of the candy bar. I'll save the rest, because the others, when they awaken, can share what's left.

As I struggle to return the candy to a pocket, I'm aware of a blast of cold wind on my face. The drag has gone around a long curve, and the wind is entering the car directly from the east. But how can there be light in the car? Or wind? We closed the door. Was it forced open by the night wind?

Now not just light and wind are coming through the opening. Snow, small flakes driven by the wind, is pouring in, already forming a long white line that, if the door isn't closed soon, will be a low wall of white. But I'm too tired, too weakened from hunger, too comfortable among the bodies. I doze again, waken again. The shaft of light, having moved and broadened, is centered on two men in the far corner of the car, sitting on the floor, their backs against the wooden wall.

The faces of both men, dark, almost black with dirt and beard, contain thick slits where the eyes should be. The slits part and eyes finally appear.

Deirdre wakes up as the others stir and sit erect. Carl and Norman, seeing the two men, say nothing. They squeeze closer against me. Slezak continues to sleep. Deirdre stands and stretches, her breath frosty mist. Bending forward, she lets her long red hair fall free and massages her scalp with both hands.

"Lordy, girl, what a head of hair."

Deirdre stiffens. At the sight of the two men, she drops back between Carl and me, her long red hair quickly stuffed inside the collars of shirts and sweaters.

"Kids," one of the two men mutters, as he might say "skunks" or "snakes."

"Where'd you kids get on?" the other 'bo asks, his voice hoarse but almost civil, almost friendly.

Slezak, awake finally, and aware of the fear among his friends, whispers, "Don't let them think they've got you cowed."

"New York," I say. "Thirty-fourth."

"Where ya headed?"

"Altoona."

"About twelve minutes," the 'bo says.

"Don't tell them about Hoagley," the darker of the two men says. He is not pleased at our presence, that's clear. He chuckles after he speaks. A thin scar line visible now on cheek and chin, where no beard grows, is too smooth, too glossy to hold dirt.

"Why not? Hells bells, I got two kid brothers and two kid sisters. They could be freezin' here. Right, mates?" He smiles at us.

"But they ain't," the scarface says.

The hoarse voice asks if we have the makings.

I nudge Carl, who digs inside his padding and comes up with a cigarette. He tosses it the length of the car. It's caught deftly by the glum one, who lights it, inhales, puffs twice more, and passes it to his buddy.

"Got any eats?" I ask.

The hoarse-voiced 'bo shakes his head. "There's a jungle nearby. Got anything to give?"

"No, we don't have anything."

"Well," Scarface says, chuckling, "I guess you don't get."

Norman whispers to me that we might offer a small bit of cash in lieu of givings. He even begins to reach inside his clothes, but my nudge stops him.

"We'll find something," I promise.

"How long you been hittin' the drags, mates?" He sounds like a frog croaking.

"Six, seven months," I say.

Scarface snickers. "Babes in the woods."

"Who's Hoagley? A bull?"

"The meanest bull this side of the Mississippi. He's got a club three feet long, and he goes for the head and kidneys. Kids, men, women, he treats them equal."

Carl turns his head so the men won't see his lips move. "Whatta you think, Willy?" He slides closer, as if the feel of my body will assure protection.

"I don't trust them," Slezak says. He transfers a large switchblade from his pants pocket to his sock.

"You have another one?" Deirdre asks.

"Yeah, a smaller one."

"Let me carry that," Deirdre says. "I might need it more than you will." And she fits the switchblade into her jacket.

"Don-don't worry," Norman says. "There won't b-be any trouble. Will there, Willy?"

"Maybe not for you," Deirdre says.

"F-for you either. We c-can run f-faster."

"I don't run," Slezak says.

"You ain't me," Deirdre says. "Old Scarface spooks me. But I sure wish we had something for the jungle. I'm hungry. If it means food, I'd be willing to take a chance with the jungle."

"I c-could sure st-stand a hot f-fire."

"I don't know," I say. "I've been to lots of jungles with my brother. If we didn't have anything they still fed us. But they know the way there. We don't. Frog Voice sounds O.K., but I don't know about Scarface. What do you think, Carl?"

Carl considers the question and then shrugs. "Whatever you say, Willy."

The freight begins to slow down. The engine howls through the wind, informing anyone interested that its speed for the next few minutes is to be progressively reduced. The two 'boes leave their corner, move to the doorway, and heave the heavy door open. The gravel-voiced 'bo looks back at us as he squints into the snow.

"I was you, mates, I wouldn't stay aboard much longer. There's a water tower ahead. That's Hoagley's hangout."

With that, he lowers himself feet first until his upper torso rests on his forearms. His body drops lower. Still gripping with his hands, he lets his feet touch ground. He runs in the direction the freight is traveling. Then he's free, running on the cinders, away from the car. Scarface follows. He too disappears.

"Let's go," I say. "We have to get food."

One by one we leave the car, repeating the movement of the two veteran 'boes. Down onto the elbows, feet lower and lower, running at the first touch of solid ground, running faster while alert for any switch or signal assembly that might smash our bodies, running faster to match the speed of the freight, freeing the body slowly. Then, away from the car, still running. Slower. Stop.

I'm sure of the abilities of everyone in Lackawanna, but after every run I look back and check the number of upright bodies, check the faces. As always they are there. I've taught them well.

The two 'boes, observing, stand at the side of the tracks, ankle deep in snow, and when we approach, even Scarface nods when the gravel-voiced 'bo tells us we sure aren't greenhorns.

"Handler," the friendlier 'bo tells Scarface, "tell the brothers I'm bringing five guests. I'm gonna teach 'em how to get whatever's gotta be got. Come on, boys. You too, sis."

5

The 'bo leads us along the tracks, the fences always at our right.

"Never do nothin' within a mile of the jungle," the 'bo advises us. "You gotta protect yourself and your brothers."

At the sound of a cackling hen the 'bo stops, forefinger to his lips. He leaves the tracks, climbs the low bank, and stands for a moment against the wall of a board shack. He nods, and after signaling for silence, motions us to come join him. I climb the bank, the rest follow. The snow filters through the three pairs of trousers I'm wearing and in between trousers and shoes and down into my socks. Norman, with his persistent aversion to cold, returns to the track, content to observe. Just the thought of snow is enough to give Norman the shivers.

The 'bo tests each board in the fence until he finds one loose enough to remove. He pries slowly, so the screech of nails is as muted as possible. It's easier, with the opening, to get at the neighboring boards.

"Keep an eye on me," he says as he crawls through the opening.

Hunched over, in case someone should be gazing out of the windows of the house, he waddles through the snow to the shack. He pulls a door open and snakes his way over the sill. He reappears a moment later, fixes the door partly open, and waddles back to the opening in the fence, dropping grains of corn he could have collected only inside the shack. There is a trail of corn on top of the snow now, leading from the open door to the opening in the fence.

One hen appears. Another. Two more hop to the ground, walking gingerly through the snow, which the weight of the 'bo's body has packed down. They peck their way along the corn trail, oblivious to any distraction, up to and through the opening and into the 'bo's waiting hands. He quickly and efficiently wrings each neck before the hen can cluck its surprise or fright.

When we have four chickens in hand and no more hens appear, the 'bo replaces the boards and secures them as well as he can with his fist. Back on the tracks and leading us, he chuckles when Deirdre says this is the first time she has ever stolen anything.

"This is how you get your givin's," the 'bo says.

Deirdre is still troubled, as are the rest of us. Begging for handouts and lying to social workers and snitching bread from a market is one thing, but stealing from someone who is probably poor and counting on the chickens and eggs . . .

"Hey," the 'bo says, "are you hungry?"

"I'm so hungry, I'm weak. My legs are shaking."

"Sister, you gotta survive. You can't live on snow. And the closest free lunch is Altoona, a hundred bulls from here. I figure it this way: The country can't give me a job, I live any way I can. I had my own chickens once. And cows. Lost everything. Well, if I'm a criminal, they can take the blame."

He reaches into a pocket and removes three eggs and, from another pocket, four more.

"He feeds his hens lotsa oyster shell, mates. They didn't break. When was the last time you had an egg?"

"About a month ago," I admit.

"Can I have one?" Deirdre asks.

The 'bo places an egg in her hand. She keeps it against her cheek. Her eyes close. "Herbie loved eggs."

In single file, Lackawanna follows the 'bo back down the tracks. The frozen gravel on the embankment shatters under our feet as we descend, but the path through the brush, packed solid, leads us into a clearing filled with a small city of boxes and blankets and canvases and branches arranged to serve as shelters. The four shelters encircling the roaring fire have received more attention than others. Roofs of cardboard covered with branches are new enough to be firm, still resisting the weight of the increasing snow pack. Extra coats and jackets and blankets and towels are draped on posts and buttoned or pinned or roped together to form sleeping quarters open to the roaring fire.

One of the more ingenious 'boes has devised a series of logs and wires that suspend two large pots over the flames. Five men sit on boxes, soaking in the red warmth, encouraging a sixth man who is tending the pots, a stocky, one-armed 'bo apparently charged with producing the evening's meal.

Two of the men are in their forties or fifties, but the others are in their twenties. Most of them welcome Lackawanna and the gravel-voiced 'bo, but it is the appearance of the chickens that brings cheers from all. The eggs are passed around and admired as if they are precious gems.

In a few minutes two of the chickens are plucked and disemboweled and in the pot, whole. The other two are hacked to pieces, speared with pointed sticks, and angled into the heat above the coals. The barbecued pieces are consumed first, and rapidly, and what is left of the bones is tossed into the pot. There are reminiscences and laughter and stories and jokes while we wait for the stew. Unable to reject the goodwill, we all begin to relax.

When cans and cups and jelly glasses and chipped bowls appear, to be filled with the stew, the clamor settles. Attention has to be given this important moment. The gravel-voiced 'bo makes sure each of us has seconds and thirds. Deirdre, her face glowing with contentment, and Norman and Slezak volunteer to clean up.

The other 'boes lie back to smoke cigarettes rolled from tobacco two of the younger men willingly distribute. Deirdre and I are not only stuffed, we're warm and drowsy.

"Pick up some sleep," Carl tells Deirdre. "I'll do your job."

Deirdre tries to protest, but Carl will not hear her, and after one more brief effort she gives in, stretches out near the fire, and settles herself on the sheets of cardboard that do not quite protect her from the wet ground.

The talk picks up again with a story about Hoagley and his killing of a 'bo the week before. The narrator knows—he's gotten it firsthand from a warthog, a trainmaster—that Hoagley received a bonus of fifty dollars from the railroad and another twenty-five from the chief of police. A pipe-smoking 'bo says it's logical.

"Read your history," he says. "It's all there. When times are bad, the police are under pressure. Sure, some of the cops might sympathize with workers or hoboes, but they've gotta keep the workers and other undesirables from the throats of the capitalists. Cops and the militia. You think the cops and the militias are there to protect the poor? I'm talkin' from experience, mind you. And history. I've read the history books. Who pays their wages, the cops' and the militias'? The rich. That's who. So you think they're gonna protect *us*? Use your heads, brothers."

One of the younger 'boes disputes the pipe smoker's charges, saying the cops are only doing their jobs.

"They're workers too."

"Yeah, sure, brother. Workers with guns, goons hired by the bosses to control the masses. Why don't they turn their guns on the common enemy, their enemy and the enemy of the masses, the rich bosses? The way those farmers are doin' right now in Kansas and North Dakota? Huh? Why? Because they are the capitalists' private army."

Another 'bo, a young one again, waves a deprecating hand at the pipe-smoking 'bo.

"Times have changed. You're one of those radicals, one of those International Workers of the World geeks. Right? No wonder you're called Wobblies—you're wobblin' away. Fadin' away."

The old Wobblie leaps up and throws his battered hat to the ground and stomps it into the mud, but he also stomps his pipe, which fell from his mouth when he leaped up.

"It isn't the times that have changed," he shouts, outraged and still stomping, to the delight of his audience. "It's young idiots like you who don't care about all those who came before you and made such sacrifices so the workers livin' now can have a better life."

Scarface, who has been staring across the fire at the sleeping Deirdre, interrupts to ask, "This is a better life?"

The others laugh, and one 'bo who's been smoking a cigar offers the old Wob the stub.

"It's healthier for you than a pipe."

The old Wobblie smiles, and, calmed down, he sits on a log.

"Ah, I'm an old dinosaur. In another ten years me and the brothers like me, men who fought the good fight, we'll be extinct. Like the brontosaurus."

The talk begins to die. A few of the 'boes settle down to sleep. Partly because of the silence and partly because it's necessary to hold at bay the hunger of memory, the hovering face of Ward, I speak out.

"I got a buddy around here somewhere," I say. "A 'bo big as a house. My little brother's with him. I've gotta get an important message to him."

Every head comes up, every eye is on me. The silence is no longer dull. It is charged, the way the air is charged just before a storm. The gravel-voiced 'bo breaks the spell.

"You askin' a question?"

"Well, I wonder if anyone's seen them."

I'm aware of Deirdre stirring. She sits up to receive the important news.

Feeling the cold, I stretch my hands toward the fire. I do not repeat the question. Deirdre whispers that we ought to leave. Carl and Slezak and Norman, having completed their work and returned to the fire, agree.

Scarface is sitting opposite us, on the other side of

the fire, near one of the younger men, muttering something to him and receiving a muttered response. The younger man is also staring at Deirdre now.

"Hey, sister," Scarface says, "let's see that red hair."

The younger 'bo joins in. "Come on, Red, let's see it."

I rise, saying we'll be going now. The others also rise, to follow me. Carl leads the way, and Norman follows him, with Deirdre next. They're followed by me and Slezak. Deirdre pretends to be casual about the way she closes the collars of the jackets about her throat.

The young man stands, as does Scarface, and they move to intercept us. Slezak, on rising, has collected a rock that helped support the barbecue apparatus. As we move forward, he says, "Get ready."

The young 'bo grabs for Deirdre but drops at her feet before he can touch her. He rises to his hands and knees, shaking his head as if trying to understand why a bell is ringing in his skull. Slezak swings his rock again. Scarface grabs at Deirdre, leaps back, the old scar reopened, flowing red.

We run then, tripping over roots and falling and rising again, and we continue running, our hands and faces whipped by branches and our clothes covered with snow shaken from the bushes. We make it to the embankment, where Deirdre stops. We gather about her. She is still holding her knife. She looks away as she holds out her hand, letting Slezak take the knife. Her teeth are chattering. "What did I do? Oh God, what did I do?"

"You saved yourself," Slezak says. "That's what you did."

"I'm scared." Her whole body is shaking.

"Everyone come closer," I say. "We have to stay warm." We hold tightly to each other.

Slezak's chuckle does not lighten the tension. "They thought they had us. You were somethin', Deirdre."

"I've never hurt anyone before."

"It's easy after the first time," Slezak says. "Hey, Norman, how'd you like that? How'd you do, partner?"

"I b-bit someone."

Carl, who's holding on to Norman, shakes him playfully. "You bit me. I wondered who had my hand in their mouth."

I remind Carl that we're one for all and all for one.

Deirdre rubs her hand across the front of her clothes. If I knew the words I'd join Deirdre as she intones, "Hail Mary, full of grace, the Lord is with thee. . . ."

6

Remembering too well the stories we've heard about Hoagley, Lackawanna avoids the yards. Slezak regrets our caution.

"Hoagley. Who's afraid of Hoagley? He ain't no lion or bear. He's human."

"Who's af-afraid? M-me."

"I don't want to meet him," I admit. "Why go looking for trouble? We've got enough already."

"If we met him and he said run, I'd run all right. I'd run right at him."

Carl shakes his head, puzzled. "You talk like you want to get yourself killed. Why?"

"Y-yeah. Why? If we're really one f-for all and all f-for one, we all oughta ag-agree, I guess. We oughta l-let ourselves g-get k-killed, too. Not m-me."

"Ah, whatta you want? You wanta live forever?"

"Y-yeah. You b-bet. If you c-could promise me I'd be warm the rest of m-my l-life by f-fighting Hoagley, I'd f-fight him right n-now."

Deirdre sighs. "Oh Lord, I'm so tired of hearing about fighting. I'm tired."

Winter has attacked the Allegheny Mountains, and now, as Lackawanna finds its way through the outskirts of town, there seems to be nothing to talk about.

Deirdre, in the lead, kicks the snow as she walks. The collar of her jacket, under her heavy coat, is turned up to protect her throat and ears. Two wool scarves are wrapped several turns over her head and around the neck and collar. She could not possibly be identified as a girl. Walking with slow deliberation, head down, she resembles in every way one of the boys behind her.

"I thought we'd find Herbie today," she says. "I wish I was back in New York, with Herbie."

Perhaps in an effort to distract her, Carl agrees. "I miss New York noise. I couldn't ever live in the country like this."

Slezak snickers. "This ain't country. Altoona's a

city. You ever hear of the Horseshoe Curve? It's famous. It's right around here somewhere."

Carl is far from convinced. "That doesn't make it a city. Listen, you hear any city noises?"

"Well, we're j-just at the edge of the c-city."

Carl persists, now that Norman has supported him. "You stand like this at the edge of New York City, and it's like being in a football stadium when Fordham plays. After we find Herbie, I'm getting back to New York City and I'm never leaving again."

I give in to my own melancholy. "I keep thinking of our basement. That furnace. You're a genius, Carl. We would have frozen there if it hadn't been for you. How about you, Deirdre? You want to live in New York forever?"

"I could live in Podunk if Herbie was with me."

"F-first thing I'm g-gonna do, I'm g-gonna sleep in front of that f-furnace for t-two days. How long we g-got till summer?"

"Spring's gotta come first, Norm." Carl laughs and pushes Norman into a snow-shrouded bush. "Remember? It's winter, then spring, *then* summer."

The houses near the railroad yards wear the forbidding gloom all such wood-frame houses wear in all such coal or railroad towns, where few families have money for coal that might be purchased, should coal even be available. A flat grayness seems to have been spray painted over every color that has at one time or another been on wall or trellis or picket fence or window frame. The occasional shop or store in which boards do not seal doors or windows contains shelves in gray rooms that offer nothing but gray dust for sale.

Two boys are going door to door trying to sell day-old newspapers and month-old magazines for half price. When they meet us on the sidewalk, there is only momentary suspicion. After preliminary probing the two groups relax, recognizing each other as fellow victims. The two boys offer important details about the town: the location of the missions, the best areas for panhandling, for finding food, for used clothes, for odd jobs. They lead us to the Salvation Army mission, and in the process, we compare our troubles.

One of the boys, who has a severe cold, keeps sniffing and spitting and coughing. He pulls a bottle from one of his many pockets every few minutes and takes large swallows. He gargles before each swallow. "Cough medicine," he says, with a wink of one heavy-lidded eye. "Snake-bite medicine, too. Altoona's filled with snakes. My name's Mike, but you guys call me Mickey."

The other boy, Paul, carries himself as if he might

be displaced nobility. Tall, slim, pale, he manages, in his shabby clothes as well as by his manners, to display a certain elegance.

"My father was an engineer. He built bridges."

No one asks why the son of an engineer who built bridges is, like the rest of us, cold and hungry and wandering the streets. It is taken for granted that if Paul wants the information made public, he'll pick the time and place it's done.

"Two years now," Mickey says. "We been goin' from Altoona to Johnstown to Hollidaysburg to Altoona for two years."

Paul adds a few facts, his voice clipped but with almost perfect enunciation. "We cadge enough back-door food—"

"Grub," Mickey corrects him.

"We cadge enough back-door food and mission treats to survive, but by adding rabbits and opossum and muskrat, well, we eat pretty good. Most of the time."

Carl's face turns pale green. "Muskrat? Is it . . . ?"

"Sure. We trap them in fields, near streams."

"M—muskrats? Are they rats?"

"Sure. But they aren't half bad. Roasted, they taste like chicken. If you hold your nose."

After every three or four words, Mickey coughs and spits in the snow. Between seizures of coughing and nose blowings they laugh and jostle each other like young animals.

No, in response to Deirdre's question, neither of them has seen a big 'bo hauling a slave.

"That kind of 'bo," Mickey says, "will be a loner. He'll stay away from missions, where the Sally people or the church leaders would toss him out or turn him over to the bulls. Then *they'll* grab the kid for salvation. Hey, a kid like that, rescued from a jocker like that, he'll probably be so grateful, he'll join the church and become a missionary. And eat and drink so well, he'll be over two hundred pounds before he's fifteen. Any gandy dancers or cinder dicks or miners—especially the miners—who see a monster like that big 'bo, they'll probably stretch his nose—yeah, his nose!—out on a rail and let a drag run it over."

Cinder dicks, we know, are simply bulls. Gandy dancers are railroad workers who keep the ties and rails in shape. I wonder about them being angry, or willing to help. There aren't too many Mr. Stevensons around, employed or unemployed.

Paul informs Lackawanna that there is a gang from Cleveland that comes to Sally's sometimes. "Those are the guys to ask. You guys headin' west? Yeah? Well, you oughta meet that Cleveland gang."

Deirdre is interested. "Will they be at the Salvation Army tonight?"

"Probably, yeah."

"We'll be there. Right, Willy?"

"Right. We'll be there."

Deirdre registers first at Sally's. Each of us receives a slip with a number identifying name and age. A formality, the well-scrubbed woman in stiff black wool says. So they'll have a record of the number of transients served.

Everyone is given a bowl of soup for lunch and then a special gift of two slices of bread not quite stale enough to taste rancid. We're also given cards for supper. Slezak says, after the insubstantial snack, that he might eat his supper card. If they sprinkle salt and pepper on it, he'll show them.

"I've already eaten my c-card and I'm ready to st-start on Carl's."

Carl, without so much as a grin, pretends to hide his card inside his clothes for safekeeping.

Before we can be assured of supper, we have to work two hours that afternoon, in addition to the hour to be spent listening to sermons and singing hymns. Sweeping, peeling spuds, washing dishes, scrubbing pots. Deirdre, her hair piled up beneath her peaked cap, has succeeded in passing herself off as a boy.

After the locals receive their supper rations, Lackawanna and other transients are permitted through the line. Some of the people sit on the floor, some lean against the walls, others pack the benches on either side of the long tables.

Supper that night is identified as stew. The liquid contains bits of tripe and meat crumbs minute enough to pass as flakes of pepper. There is also a bowl of beans thickened with mashed potatoes.

At the benches on either side of Lackawanna's table are Mickey and Paul and four other boys, all in their early teens. One, Specks, is black. His neck is thick, with cords of muscle on each side. The rest of his body is probably heavily muscled as well, but like everyone else in the steaming fetid room, he has hidden his body with accumulations of cloth. If he continues eating like this, he complains, shaking his head at the material on his plate, they're going to get him skinny and white.

Specks is the only one at the table who seems to be free of coughs and sniffles and chapped lips and a running nose. Mickey points a fork at Specks.

"I think Specks saw your 'bo."

Deirdre gasps,

and I drop my spoon and Norman stops shivering.

"Whadda you hear?" Slezak says.

Specks' glasses are so thick that his eyes are pools of spinning color changing hue and direction every time he blinks.

"Where?" Deirdre finally manages to blurt out. "When? Was Herbie O.K.?"

"I was tellin' Mickey. Him and Paul was askin' around, and I was tellin' them, yeah, I saw them." He tries the food, shakes his head, grimaces, and pushes the plate aside. "This mornin' I was in Johnstown jes standin' in a store, in the doorway. I been watchin' this bakery truck. Waitin'. I keep followin' it. Finally this driver, he forgets, like I knew he would sooner or later. He parks his truck and he goes in a store and he leaves the back of the truck open. Before I can lift my foot, there's this little guy, he pops up from nowhere, like out from a manhole or somethin'. He's up and in and outa that truck so fast, I wondered if I saw what I thought I saw."

"Was he small? Pale? With freckles?"

"Yeah, he was small. And wearin' a red tassle cap. With these glasses I can't tell is someone pale or dark or got freckles. Not if they're fifteen, twenty feet away like he was. Up close I can tell if a butterfly's a he or a she, but I don't see butterflies in winter."

We endure his enjoyment of his own joke.

"After he gets his arms full of cakes and bread, he shags off 'cross the street and there's this yell. He stops. He turns and comes back like one of them dolls you move with strings. Whadda you call them?"

"P-puppets," Norman says, his dark eyes bulging. "P-puppets."

"Puppets, right. He comes back like one of them puppets. Then I see this big 'bo, he's about the size of an elephant. I saw an elephant once. At a circus in Biloxi. Anyway, the big guy and the kid go 'round the corner, and that's all I see of them. You know? I never did get even a doughnut crumb outa that truck. The driver, he runs outa the store screamin' and shakin' both fists, and I stand there tastin' air."

"Johnstown," I say.

"That's where it was." Specks nods several times. "But I bet they're outa there by now. I bet they was outa there on the first drag. The driver was screamin' for the bulls when he runs in the store. I hightailed it, 'cause the bulls 'round here, they catch a black man, they can be mean. You ask me, I think they're all Hoagley's cousins. I'm bettin' they're over the next three hills by now."

Slezak suggests we forgo the beds, for which we have reservations. Carl says it's up to me, whatever I say is fine with him. Norman agrees, though he's been talking incessantly about the night's promise of sleep between two sheets and under blankets in a warm room.

"Look," Deirdre says, "you want to stay and get a good night's sleep, do it. This ain't your fight."

I almost shout. "Carl, throw *The Three Musketeers* at her. We promised to stick together. We belong to each other. Remember what you said once, Deirdre? We're a family."

"Let's go," Deirdre says. She gives Mickey her check for the bed. "Give this to someone who can use it."

The rest of Lackawanna follow suit, though Norman gazes at his bed check as if it were a pet. He sighs deeply.

Mickey and Paul remind Lackawanna that if we need help, there are always 'boes coming to Altoona. "Send a message to Sally's. Tell them to ask for Mickey and Paul. Everyone here knows Mickey and Paul."

7

Deciding to give Hoagley a wide berth, Lackawanna walks for several miles until we are a fair distance from the yards. We wait near a water tower, knowing that sometime soon a freight is sure to stop or slow down for the engine to take on water.

We wait about fifteen minutes.

There are other 'boes in the car, including kids, but no one has seen a big 'bo with a kid in tow.

The next morning Deirdre charms a brakie, and after he hears her story he goes into a cluster of bunkhouses occupied by crewmen waiting to return to wherever they came from the day before. None of them has seen a small freckle-faced boy with a big 'bo.

"They're heading west," I say. "They have to be."

For the next two days Lackawanna too moves west, asking, asking, and receiving the same answer. No, no one has seen a big jocker with a freckle-faced boy.

Cold, hungry, almost ready to admit defeat, Lackawanna nails a drag into Youngstown.

We've experienced enough to know that the bitter cold can freeze fingers—an event which, for a 'bo, is a direct and rapid passage to hell. And so when Slezak meets a switchman who gives him his very own work gloves, leather burnished to a high gloss, Slezak knows the man can be trusted. In fact, the switchman declares his sympathies for all hoboes, especially the girls.

"The way those young girls have gotta live just about tears my heart apart."

The switchman shares his thermos of coffee with Slezak, who hasn't had coffee with cream and sugar for weeks. After hearing the story about Herbie and the big 'bo, the switchman advises Slezak which freight specifically should be caught and which car in the freight and, if we're fixed in our minds to move west, where exactly to catch it. If a bull (he says "detective") named Hoagley, who roams the line from Erie to Cleveland to Youngstown to Steubenville, threatens Lackawanna, Slezak is to tell the bull they're friends of Pennington. J. H. Pennington. "That's my monicker."

Slezak should also tell Hoagley that J. H. Pennington has suggested—no, demanded!—that the kids be invited into the crummy to sleep and eat. The switchman, tall and slim in his clean bib overalls, has the silvery-gray hair and fine silver mustache of a matinee idol. He sends Slezak away with a bag of cinnamon rolls to distribute among Lackawanna.

Like dark-furred bears we wait in a snow-filled ditch near the siding Pennington designated. Faces up, tongues out, we catch the falling snowflakes. For the moment I forget the reason I'm here in this cold, alien country. I used to hold on to the playground fence and lean back, eyes closed, my mouth open to catch the falling snowflakes on my tongue. The flakes, like sugar crystals, would strike and melt and leave, for just a fraction of a second, a taste of heaven. I got ten, a child would call. I got twelve. Fourteen. Not interested in records, I would not take time to count or shout, but as I do now, I'd taste the fine dissolvable diamonds thrown from the heavens by a God who understood what children need in order to play games, in order to have fun.

Our legs encased in paper and wool, our bodies puffed with layers of clothing, with muffs and scarves protecting ears and throats, we wait. We listen to the calls of other engines, the drum of other freights. No one would dare permit mention now of family or home or school days, our plundered childhood. For the moment the harsh winter night is past, present, and future.

"It's almost . . ." Slezak says, and then he is silent. No one urges him on, though all of us know the unstated word is *Christmas*.

Fortunately the freight rolls by at that moment, so we are occupied in counting the six gondolas, the eight tank cars, and the nine refrigerator cars. Reefers, the 'boes call them. Forget all those cars, J. H. Pennington advised Slezak. Next should be—and there are, just as the admirable friend informed us—the three empty boxcars, two labeled Bessemer & Lake Erie and one Baltimore and Ohio. We should wait even longer, we should not be tempted. The engine will push the collection onto a siding, where three gondolas will be waiting.

"The first group'll ride to the joint," J. H. Pennington had said.

"What's that mean?" Slezak had asked.

"Means they'll be coupled."

The performance goes off as predicted, to the very second. Now—as the puffing engine tugs the new assembly back onto the main track, and the brakie, after shifting the switch, walks on down the line—now is the time to climb into one of the empty boxcars.

Perfect. We come up out of the ditch and into the car without so much as a grunt. The floor is covered with a thick pad of fresh hay. Carl actually wrestles with Norman, tossing the hay into the air and covering Norman until his words sound like the bleating of a lamb. When have we ever had, when will we ever again have, such comfort?

"Hey," Carl says, "you think maybe J. H. Pennington is actually Santa Claus?"

Deirdre, glancing through the partially open door, notices that instead of moving west, out of the yard, as expected, the drag is returning to the yards. It no sooner halts than the door is rolled open farther. A tall skinny man with a red canvas hunting cap on his head and a red canvas hunting jacket stands there, grinning. He carries a shotgun under his arm.

"Out," he says. "Git out. I mean *out!*"

"We're f-friends of J. H. P-Pennington," Norman manages.

"I said to git out and I mean *out!*" He lifts the shotgun to a ready position and we all rush to leap out and, as further ordered, to line up at the side of the freight.

"We are," I try, "we're friends of J. H. Pennington. He said—"

"Yeah," Carl adds, as if his voice is finally required to add emphasis, to more clearly amplify the significance of that special friendship with J. H. Pennington. "Yeah, Mr. Pennington said we might even be able to ride in the crummy."

The bull snickers. "J. H. Pennington strikes again." He lifts the muzzle of his shotgun. "You," he says to Carl, "what are you lookin' so sour about?"

Carl throws his hands in the air. "Don't shoot me. I didn't do . . ."

The terror in Carl's voice seems to please the man. He tells Carl to step up, to tell him his name. Instead, Carl only becomes more fixed in his stare, in his quivering.

"Come on over here, boy."

"Please, mister." It is Deirdre. When the man turns to her, Carl, for whatever reason, runs. He completes about three steps. The bull whirls and brings the shotgun barrel down across Carl's shoulder.

Carl screams. He drops to his knees, groaning.

The rest of us, shocked at the cruelty of that man who called himself J. H. Pennington, do not move. We ignore the freight now rolling behind us, slowly picking up speed.

"I've been roustin' bums all day," the bull says. "Now I'm goin' home." He holds out his hand, palm up. "Fifty cents from each of you."

I tell Norman to give him the money.

Norman holds out a single dollar bill. When the man grabs Norman's wrist and jerks him forward, bringing a shriek from Norman, Slezak, bellowing, leaps at the bull, striking the man's chest with his head. The shotgun falls to the ground, on its muzzle. It remains upright and then flops over, dropping onto the tracks beneath the freight. The sound of the weapon's destruction cannot be heard above the sounds of the iron wheels and the hooting of the engine's steam whistle.

Slezak stands over the man, his knife in his hand.

"Don't," Deirdre pleads. "Don't do it, Sleze."

The man's hunting cap has been knocked from his head, and as he kneels there he looks like a child about to be punished. He is making strange noises in his throat, the noises a child makes when he tries hard not to be caught weeping.

"Slezak," Deirdre pleads. "For me. Don't."

"O.K.," Slezak says. "Get up. Get outa here."

The man stands and runs. After a few seconds he is only a blob in the snow, and then the blob vanishes in the darkness.

Deirdre kneels at Carl's side, weeping. "Carl, oh Carl."

Leaning forward, supporting himself on his left hand, Carl can only whimper. His right arm still hangs free.

"Oh my God," Deirdre says. "I think your arm's busted."

"I'm gonna be sick," Carl says. "Don't look."

But Deirdre and Slezak support him, Deirdre with her arms under and around Carl's chest and back and Slezak cupping Carl's head in his hands.

"Here," I say, "swallow some snow. That'll help."

"You shoulda let me finish him off," Slezak says.

"No. There'd be cops everywhere. We'd never save Herbie."

"B-boy," Norman says. "I'm g-g-glad you're my buddy. Thanks, Sleze."

Slezak nods and looks away, finding it difficult to accept the flattery.

Carl begins to weep. He tries to apologize, but the pain, the nausea, the humiliation, the exhaustion, are too much.

Deirdre turns to me. "We gotta get help."

"Come on, Norman, we'll find someone." Slezak pulls Norman into action, and they hurry down the track on which the freight has just been traveling.

After almost an hour of appeals that bring more curses than support, they find a man in dark greasy overalls, a pin displayed on his bib and another, the same pin, on his black cap.

"I'm a snake," the man says, when he arrives. He points to the large S on the pins. "A switchman." He taps the pin, almost caressing it. "This is the Switchmen's Union of North America."

The switchman is off duty, on his way home, but he leads us across the tracks and into a shanty, where he makes a sling for Carl's arm. He finds a bottle of aspirin tablets in a drawer of a littered desk, gives two to Carl, and stuffs the bottle in one of Carl's pockets.

"I know the man," he says. "Hoagley. I promise you, he'll get his."

The snake returns home late for supper that night, because he spends the next hour getting Lackawanna to a streetcar and rides with us to the hospital.

Carl's clavicle is broken badly and he is also in shock. In addition, he is so weak from exposure and malnutrition that he'll end up with pneumonia, the doctor says, if he leaves the hospital. He'll have to remain for a week, maybe two.

"Think we ought to give up?" Slezak asks.

We are standing in a bread-and-soup line. Forty or fifty men are ahead of us and another forty or fifty behind.

"You all go back," Deirdre says. "I'll go on by myself."

"If you go on, I do too," Slezak says.

"We're t-together," Norman says. "How many t-times do I have to t-tell you, Deirdre?" His big dark eyes are moist. He draws himself up and scowls, looking like a very old, very wise man.

"Thanks, Norman. You guys are the best friends I'll ever have. Ever, ever."

"We'll always b-be t-together. Even when we're old and m-married and have our own f-families and jobs."

Deirdre stares at him, mouth open, as if he's just informed her that the month is April and the light is darkness. She bursts out laughing and throws her arms around him. Slezak and I join her. We stand there, knotted in each other's arms, laughing hysterically. Several men step out of the line to try to see what, under such conditions, can elevate people to such happiness.

We sleep that night in the back of a canvas-covered truck that has apparently been deserted in the narrow alley where it has broken down. We huddle together, blanketed with a layer of newspapers six inches thick.

"You know," Norman says, "I think I'm wa-warm, b-but I'm not sure."

"You're warm," Slezak says.

"How d-do you know, S-Sleze?"

"Your nose ain't blue."

"You c-can't see my nose. It's d-dark."

"Didn't anyone ever tell you? When your nose is cold, it glows in the dark."

Norman laughs. "Aw, you're f-f-full of . . . aw, phooey."

8

Because the Youngstown hospital caters to Welfare cases and transients, our appearance in the lobby and on the floors is not unusual. Most of the patients are elderly, victims of diseases associated with age complicated by neglect. Drugs and medicines are in short supply. There is an inadequate crew of doctors, and those available are exhausted and almost as depressed as their patients, who, because they've been admitted, must be seriously ill. Patients who can breathe and are lukewarm and can wriggle their toes are expected to find refuge in missions or flophouses.

Slezak leans against the foot of the bed.

"Hey! Look! I've never seen such white sheets. I just might go out and break a leg. All those magazines. Nothin' to do but eat and sleep and get fat. This is the life, Carl."

Carl, unimpressed by our strained efforts at humor, complains that he's going to be left behind, that we'll never see each other again. Deirdre says she'll try to let him know where we are. She has a nurse write the address of the hospital on a slip of paper and gives the slip to me, advising me to keep it in the same pocket that has the slip with Stevenson's number.

"Oh, my God!"

I slap my forehead. "I forgot, too. We were supposed to call him."

"We better get to a phone now," Deirdre says, starting to leave. She returns, takes Carl's hand, and promises to return right after we talk to Stevenson.

Even though Carl's hair has been cut almost to the scalp and he has been bathed not once but twice, he is despondent.

"I promise," Deirdre says.

"I'll m-make her c-come b-back."

"Hey," Slezak says, "you think we'd leave one of our musketeers without a good-bye?"

I hold Carl's foot. "You'll be here until your shoulder heals. That's going to be a week or two, the doctor says. So you aren't going anywhere. At least not today. We'll be back in an hour. Maybe two."

We find a telephone at the bus terminal. I dial the number, but don't have the correct change for a long-distance call. Norman goes to the clerk at the grilled window and returns with a handful of quarters, nickels, and dimes. This time the call goes through.

"Stevenson ain't here. He's off for a couple of days. Gone home to Ohio. A death in the family."

"Has he left any messages for me? My name's Willy. My little brother—"

"Oh, you're the young hobo whose brother was snatched by—"

"That's me. Did Stevenson leave any messages for me?"

"No messages. But I know Stevenson's been talkin' to people in Chicago. He'll be back, let's see the schedule here, he'll be back the twenty-second. Tuesday the twenty-second. Be sure to call before Thursday, because he'll probably be takin' off for the holidays." And the line's dead.

Deirdre has followed my conversation, so she knows there's been no contact. She paces back and forth, stomping her feet, pulling her hair.

"Why'd I forget?"

"We were running," I say. "We can't remember everything, Deirdre."

"I *have* to remember everything. You don't. Herbie's not your brother."

"He *is* my brother. He's almost my brother."

"Almost, yeah. But I was there when Mom and Dad brought him home. I held him and fed him and changed his diapers."

"We're together. O.K., I didn't change his diapers, but we've been hungry together and cold together, and we help each other live. You think I'm not mad? You think I don't want to kick and scream because I forgot to call? What do we do, Deirdre? There's nothing we can do except keep on. Come on." I hold her in my arms.

Slezak and Norman take their turns at trying to comfort Deirdre.

"Hey," Slezak says, "why didn't we keep our bed? It was all set up. Why? Why? Why? You could ask a thousand questions if you want to. Like Willy says, there's nothing to do but keep on."

"Y-yeah. You c-can find all sorts of reasons f-for b-blaming yourself. You ain't a m-machine. You're a human being."

Deirdre has stopped weeping. "I never used to cry. Now it seems I cry all the time. O.K., I'll do better, I'll try."

Slezak also hugs her. "We'll find Herbie. It's just *when*. Right? How soon. Right?"

"Y-yeah. Right."

Carl is sitting up peering down the hall in anticipation of our arrival. After we talk for a few minutes, Carl winks and motions me to the other side of the bed. I go there, passing the man in the next bed and trying not to stare. The man's head and face are covered with blood-soaked bandages.

"Take this, Willy." Carl shoves a box into my hand.

"What is it?"

"Take it. Hide it. It's chocolate candies."

"Choc—"

"Ssh. Someone brought it for the guy in the other bed. Look at him. They'll be rotten by the time he gets to eat them."

"Carl, we oughtn't to eat these. Did you steal . . . ?"

A voice shouts from beneath the bandages. "They wasn't stolen. I give 'em to him."

"Thanks, mister. O.K., we'll share them. Now we better go."

Carl drops his gaze when Deirdre says good-bye. He nods when she promises we'll return before the two weeks it'll take him to heal, but he cannot deny his gloom. Deirdre leans over and kisses his cheek.

"You k-kissed him. That's the f-first t-time I ever

saw you k-kiss anyone. I forgot you were a g-girl."

"I didn't forget," Deirdre says.

On the sidewalk, I look up at the sky. "It's gonna snow again."

No one seems concerned.

"Deirdre."

"Yeah, Willy?"

"I think you oughta carry these." I hand her the chocolates.

She looks at the box for a moment; then, laughing, she gives me a quick kiss on the cheek.

"Hey, t-twice in one day. Holy m-mackerel!"

Holding Norman, Deirdre kisses him. Holding Slezak, she kisses him. "It's the first time anyone ever gave me a box of candy."

We are on a drag chugging its way to Youngstown. Most of the cars are Baltimore and Ohio, but a few are Pennsylvania and several are Chesapeake, with Chessy the cat, tucked beneath a blanket, riding the sides of the cars all over the country. "Lucky c-cat," Norman says. "She sleeps all the t-time, never wakes up."

Partly because the snow has stopped and partly because the air is like early spring, the roofs and the decks are covered with 'boes. Several ride the rods out of choice, out of habit, not just out of defiance.

"You ever ride the blinds?" a young black 'bo asks us now, as the train speeds through the Ohio countryside.

I nod. "I have, but they haven't."

Slezak thrusts out his jaw. "Let's do it."

"Why?" Deirdre asks.

"Well, for one thing, it's warmer."

"L-let's do it."

"O.K.," the black 'bo says. "But we gotta wait till the drag stops or slows down so we can get up on deck. While we're waitin', let's feed." He leads us to an uninhabited corner of the car and removes a paper bag from inside his heavy coat.

"Codfish cakes," he says. "I got 'em from an old lady in Pittsburgh. An ol' white woman didn't have no more food in her kitchen than my momma does."

He grins. "But she had these." He passes two to each of us. "I chopped some wood for her, and I cleaned out her henhouse. A weasel got some of her chickens other night, so I did a little trick my daddy taught me. I collected over a hundred tin cans from her and her neighbors, cut them and flattened them and nailed them over every hole and crack in the floor. That henhouse is weaselproof now, and ratproof and polecatproof and just about personproof. The woman liked it so much, she used half her canned codfish to pay me. My name's Dixie."

About four miles east of the city, Dixie alerts us to a grade that slows every drag to near zero. Off to the side of that grade, down about a hundred yards from the tracks, is a jungle. We should pass that one by. East of Youngstown, just at the end of the long iron bridge, is another jungle. We should go there and ask for Rhode Island Red and tell him we're friends of Dixie's. He'll take care of us. Himself, Dixie, he's heading for California. We ought to go into Youngstown first, Deirdre says, to find a phone. Then go back and find Rhode Island Red.

"Grade's comin' up," Dixie says, as several 'boes rise and move toward the door. "They're gettin' off for this jungle. It's a big 'un. We can get ready, though. Now don't you li'l 'uns be scared. Riding the blinds ain't dangerous. Sometimes the engine crew, if they's in a foul mood, they throw lumps of coal at the 'boes ridin' there, but usually they worries more 'bout what's in front of them than what's behind."

We follow Dixie out of the car and up the ladder and onto the deck. As the drag begins rolling again, we follow Dixie along the decks of boxcars, down into and up out of gondolas, along the sidewalks that border the tank cars, onto the decks of other boxcars. The freight has picked up speed and is now rushing into the wind. The snow has thinned, almost stopped, but every board and piece of steel plate, and every steel rung, has to be felt for ice deposits. Three people—I cannot tell if they are men or women, though their laughter has the higher pitch that suggests girls, if not women—are balanced on the couplings. The drag is moving too fast and the cars are swaying too much for anyone to stand, so I, on my hands and knees, hold on tightly to the deck boards behind Deirdre. Suddenly the engineer, four cars forward, hits the brakes. Ahead, Dixie grabs the coat of the screaming Deirdre, and I, holding the deck with one hand, grab her trousers. Together, Dixie and I haul her back onto the deck. Flat on our bellies, squinting against the cinders hurled to the rear by the wind, we wait until the swaying eases, and then we rise and continue toward the engine.

When we reach the car right behind the engine, we climb down.

"This is the blinds," Dixie says.

"My G-God, it's warm, Willy. You c-can feel the heat f-from the engine."

Deirdre is almost weeping. "Dixie, those women . . ."

"Honey, don't ask. And for sure don't go look. Me, I'm gettin' off in Youngstown and catchin' a Chicago, Burlington and Quincy west."

"Whatta you think, Deirdre?"

"I think we ought to call Stevenson. We've been

running all over the country and haven't talked to him. Maybe . . ."

"Maybe he has some *info.*"

"Right." She smiles. "Info. We need info. Maybe we can find a phone in Youngstown."

"Then come back to the jungle?"

"You oughta do that," Dixie puts in. "Find Rhode Island Red. He's a good ol' 'bo."

Deirdre manages to smile her gratitude through the sooty heat.

9

We find a Sally's in Youngstown and wait in line for a ticket for a cot tonight. It is not too difficult to endure the one-hour sermon and the half hour of hymns. Little enough, everyone long ago agreed, to pay for comfort and food.

After a breakfast of coffee and bread, and the added luxury of margarine and jam, Lackawanna walks the streets looking for a shop or drugstore or library or post office that might have a public telephone. Most of the shops are closed, windows and doors boarded up. FOR SALE . . . GONE FISHING . . . RUN OUT OF MONEY AND FAITH . . .

We move through neighborhoods of ascending elegance until we find ourselves on a street lined with naked trees and large red brick homes. Deirdre is exasperated. We've wasted hours. We couldn't call last night, Stevenson wouldn't have been there, but today, this morning, we *have* to call. She'll find a phone if she has to roll up her eyeballs and throw a fit.

There is little visible evidence of the Depression on this street. The red brick houses remind her, Deirdre says, of photographs of Civil War mansions.

"This house here will be the one. I feel it." She removes her cap and stuffs it in a pocket. "You guys hide somewhere and wait for me. Willy, give me the paper with Stevenson's number."

"Can you read it?" The paper has begun to disintegrate. My head close to Deirdre's, I help her translate.

Once we're satisfied she can make out the numbers, Deirdre places the paper in a pocket, washes her face with snow, and dries it with her scarf. After she shakes her long red hair loose, she produces a thinly bristled hairbrush from another pocket.

"Wish me luck," she calls, as she throws her red hair back and steps high through the snow, following a recently cleared path.

In silence, openmouthed, wide-eyed, we have observed the transformation of urchin to beautiful, wistful, but self-assured young woman. Now, concealed behind a garage, we can see only the upper half of her body moving along the top of the hedgerow.

"You know," Slezak says, "I bet she does it."

Norman's teeth are chattering, but he finally clears his stammered agreement.

I shake my head, not in doubt but in admiration. "She makes me wonder sometimes."

"Wonder what?" Slezak says.

"She really ought to lead Lackawanna."

"Aw, c-come on, Willy. You g-got us t-together."

"Yeah, but she *keeps* us together."

Those qualities that impress us must also impress the woman who comes to the door. Deirdre is immediately invited into the house.

"I h-hope she's not k-kept p-prisoner in there."

Slezak begins preparing for that eventuality. "I'll break the door down. If she doesn't come out, we better go get her."

"M-maybe they'll ask her to s-stay. Would you?"

"Would I what?"

"Stay. If they asked you. It's w-warm in there. Look at the s-smoke coming out of the ch-chimney."

"Not me." Slezak slams one fist into the other. "I wanta get that big 'bo. This time . . ." He jabs and hooks the frozen air, demonstrating his intentions when he and the 'bo meet.

"I'd st-stay. For a while. I'd g-give ten thousand d-dollars to be warm again. I was n-never c-cold at home."

Slezak grips my arm. "You think they'll call the bulls?"

"She'd let us know somehow. She'd scream or something. We'd break a window and get inside and get her out before the bulls could get here. Nah, she'll be O.K."

Even my trust is about to give way when Deirdre appears at the door. How long has it been? An hour? Two hours? She comes down the path between the hedges as if she's a queen sailing a white river. Behind her, filling the doorway, a group of children, and the woman, are waving, calling. "Good-bye, Deirdre, good-bye, good-bye."

Pretending no interest whatever in the garage, Deirdre goes straight to the sidewalk and turns in the direction of the railyards. We wait until the door closes and Deirdre is on the sidewalk before we chase after her.

A queen she is, wearing a new fingertip jacket and, beneath the jacket, crisp new coveralls, the kind worn by mechanics. And red wool gloves that, as Norman notes, "C-could k-keep an ice c-cube warm."

Tightly laced shiny leather boots reach to her knees. But the most astonishing change: She *looks* clean. Not just clean, but thoroughly *purged* of dirt. "Yes," Deirdre admits, as she continues walking, "I soaked. In a bathtub. I washed my hair. In steaming hot water, perfumed. She gave me a huge thick towel."

Slezak and Norman and I drop back a few steps.

"You feel scummy?" Slezak whispers. Norman makes a face and nods.

Deirdre carries a bag over her shoulder that, under normal circumstances, would promptly reduce her to the status of a 'bo. But no 'bo ever had such an air of hygienic purity. In her wake I, like Slezak, feel not just dirty but weak. Ineffectual. Could I have done what she's accomplished at the house? I wonder.

When we stop in the backyard of one of the less sumptuous homes, and let ourselves into a shed that contains the skeletons of an old touring car and two tricycles, Deirdre opens the bag. Inside are new clothes, including skirts and blouses and sweaters, and socks, and a pair of men's shoes, and real red-flannel underwear. Real food as well, in neatly tied boxes that look like Christmas gifts: meat sandwiches with lettuce and mayonnaise, and thick cheese slices, and cupcakes with icing sprinkled with red sugar dots, and apples. And a quart jar filled with the hottest, strongest coffee any of us has ever tasted, with real cream and sugar.

"From the minute she opened the door, I had them."

We huddle together, gulping the sandwiches, passing the jar of coffee around, too excited and too pleased with ourselves to pay attention to the clouds of steam drifting about our faces.

"There were four kids. From six to twelve, maybe thirteen. Mr. Kellar works in Washington for the government. They ain't going hungry, I'll tell you. But I could see they'd have even more than they got if things were different. I kept them sort of entertained. There was a maid. I don't think I had her fooled, but she didn't let on. She heard my name, and well, I couldn't do anything wrong. Her name was Maggie and she sounded like she left Ireland yesterday. She reminded me of my grandma. I told stories. My poor old mother who's dying, my poor father coming home every evening to his hungry wife and children and after months of no job and no money and no food his jumping off the Brooklyn Bridge. By the time I finished, the house was filled halfway up the chimney with tears. Even old Maggie patted my head. I could have called anywhere in the world, if I wanted to, for nothing."

I managed to shake free of my trance. "You called Stevenson."

"I called Stevenson. Told him I was your sister. The Kellars just stood around. There I was, talking about schedules and railroads and cities, saying yes, Mr. Stevenson, thanks, Mr. Stevenson. I could have stayed even longer. They begged me. There were extra bedrooms. No, no, I have to get back to poor old Mother, who's sitting up with poor old Danny-boy, who is three years old and who's never even tasted orange juice."

Deirdre pulls four oranges out of the bag, keeps one, and tosses one to each of us. Norman sniffs his and rolls his eyes. Slezak bites into the skin, peels it, and eats the orange in three large sucking gulps. He chews the peel as if it's beefsteak, then rubs the large bulk of clothing his lean stomach hides behind.

I observe my orange for several minutes, grinning. Anyone who can produce an orange in this country, in this weather, has to be a genius.

"You're something, Deirdre. You sure are. From now on you decide things. You're our chief."

Deirdre waves my generosity aside and goes on as if no mention has been made of authority. But Slezak and Norman are nodding, seriously weighing my recommendations. They support the nomination. She would not receive more serious admiration were she Joan of Arc.

"What about Stevenson?" I ask. "Did he remember?"

"Sure he remembered. And he had some info. That's what he calls it, info. He didn't really trust me at first, but I convinced him I came from New York to join the chase."

Slezak is impressed. "You could really hear him? When you were so far apart?"

"They yelled l-loud," Norman explains. Slezak only pretends to punch Norman but, even knowing he's safe, Norman refuses to take chances. He steps behind me.

"Come on, Deirdre," I plead. "Tell us."

"O.K. Listen to this. Stevenson said the big 'bo was in Cleveland yesterday. So they're still in Ohio."

"Cleveland!"

"Yeah, but he's betting they're going west fast. As fast as they can. He beat up a brakie on The Western Maryland. The brakie ran the 'bo off a drag. He had Herbie with him. Herbie fell. The brakie caught Herbie. Then—I can't understand this—Stevenson says Herbie didn't try to get away. It was his chance. The big 'bo beat up the brakie, almost killed him, and he ran off!"

"Wh-what ab-about Herbie?"

"He ran off with the 'bo."

We try to comprehend, but it is too difficult. The implications cannot be believed.

"Maybe that brakie told a lie." Slezak cocks his right fist. "Maybe he didn't want to admit he was afraid of the 'bo."

Deirdre cannot explain. But her concerns are not important. What *is* important is the fact that we're only hours apart.

"Stevenson thinks maybe the 'bo really has Herbie scared of him, you know, sort of hypnotized. Anyway, every bull on every railroad is watching for them. City bulls, too. Stevenson says the 'bo will lay low for a while, till things cool down. Probably hide in some jungle around Cleveland. Stevenson said there's a B. & L. E. to Cleveland."

Slezak dances up, fists at the ready. "Let's go."

I make quite a show of deferring to Deirdre, waiting for her to decide. She refuses to take the lead.

"You're the chief," I say. "We're so close now, *you* oughta be in charge."

Deirdre shakes her head, stiffens, holds my eye. "You serious? You really want me to take over? It's your gang. Lackawanna's yours, Willy."

"It's *our* gang," I reply. "I was O.K. at the beginning, but now, well, I don't want to take chances. He's your brother. He's my friend, my buddy, but he's your brother, like you said. You ought to be the one who decides things now."

Deirdre stands, the burlap bag at her feet. Norman takes it from her, to carry it over his shoulder, but Slezak, in turn, pulls it out of Norman's hands. He and Norman and I stand there, staring at Deirdre, waiting.

"Let's go," Deirdre says.

A short skinny 'bo hovers over a fire he's built under a trestle. He merely glances up, squinting, as Lackawanna approaches. He is ten, eleven perhaps, but his face is the face of a tired and defeated old man.

"Yeah," he says, in answer to Deirdre's question, "Loose told me about him. He's the biggest man she ever saw."

"Who's Loose?"

"She's with Bessemer. You know those old cars down near where the junkyard used to be?"

"No. We don't live around here."

"I'll show you. I'll take you toward the place. I won't go in, but you can. Just start lookin' around the junkyard and you'll find them. They'll probably find you first."

"What's Bessemer?"

"A gang. You said you're Lackawanna? Well, they're Bessemer. But what say we stick around the fire a bit? I just got it goin'."

"Oh b-boy, yeah. J-just a b-bit."

We are no sooner through the gate, or what was once a gate, of the junkyard than three kids pop up from behind the hulks of trucks and cars that hover under the snow like shrouded tombstones. The three boys, in their early teens, move forward without the slightest suggestion of friendship. Slezak steps in front of Deirdre. He is smiling, as if pleased at the possibility that they might charge him.

The three boys, each holding a wrench in his hand, are not sure what to do. They outnumber the husky kid standing there in front of them, fists drawn up, feet set, looking very much like one of those veteran fighters pictured on the sports pages, but they have to whisper together to decide.

Lackawanna is in a room created by vehicles arranged with the precision of building blocks. Doors and fenders and bumpers and running boards lock and interlock, forming walls so thick that wind or snow cannot penetrate. Several canvases have been spread overhead as a roof, secured in some instances by ropes, in others by wires, all pitched at angles steep enough to shed snow. There is almost an air of carnival inside, with all activity—resting, sleeping, eating, card games—occurring around the glowing iron drum. The black pipe protruding from the drum twists and turns as it climbs through the second and third tiers of cars. Fifteen feet above the floor the pipe pokes through the highest canvas. Up there, where the warm air hovers, the head of a boy or a girl peers occasionally from a window of a car or truck or bus.

Near the stove a large wooden box, the size and shape of a coffin, contains lumps of coal. Around the stove, on the board floor, are bits and pieces of what might be called chairs or sofas.

Bessemer is made up of fourteen kids. At least there are fourteen who, at one time or another, make their presence known. Two, perhaps three, are girls. The leader, or the one who seems to be the leader, who does most of the talking and makes most of the recommendations, is a girl chunkier than Slezak and, it seems, as unafraid of anything that moves.

"My name's Lucy," she says when they meet, "but everyone calls me Loose."

Deirdre tells Loose and the others the details of Herbie's kidnaping and the events of the following days. After a brief discussion Deirdre is convinced that the man Loose saw was the big 'bo. But where was Herbie? Had he escaped? Had he gone back to our cellar room in New York? Could he make it, all alone? Or—and Deirdre covers her face with her hands when she considers this possibility—is Herbie dead?

Deirdre admits her fears. I begin to reassure her but stop. Reassurance is impossible.

Loose thinks our friend Stevenson is correct. Having beaten a railroad worker, the big 'bo will not be able to go near a drag for a month or two. Things are going to be hot for all 'boes. The big 'bo will have to seek out a jungle. Well, there are three jungles she knows about within a radius of ten miles. One of those three is more isolated than the other two, would promise more shelter. That's the one he'll most likely choose. She and four others from Bessemer will accompany Lackawanna to the jungle. The rest of Bessemer will stay behind and, if lucky, will build up a stash of food.

"One of the nice things about winter is you don't have to worry about food spoiling. Every car chassis in the junkyard's a refrigerator. You're lucky it ain't summer. This place would be hotter than it is cold now."

She chuckles and adds, as if it's a ploy deliberately played, "Something else. Summer or winter, social workers can't find their way through the junk. The same with cops."

That night Deirdre sleeps in the backseat of a 1929 Studebaker with its isinglass windows reinforced by several layers of cardboard. I have a Dodge, its backseat as wide and soft as any bed I've ever slept in. Slezak curls up in the backseat of a Model A Ford filled with rags. He sinks down like a stone in water.

"Just like the car my old man had. Rags and all. Except his went thirty miles an hour. Honest to God! We used to pass airplanes."

Norman sleeps in the interior of a Pierce Arrow, on top of a mound of old clothes and under four coats and three bathrobes, with the fire's warmth seeping through the walls.

"Hey, Norman," Slezak calls from his Model A, "you warm enough? You wanta race?"

"I'm n-never leaving. I'm n-never g-getting out of this limousine till I d-die."

We start for the train yards at noon. The two-fourteen B. & L. E. practically stops and waits for us to hop aboard. Then it rambles.

At five o'clock the purple light hovering above the snow lights our way—nine of us now—along the bank and down through the snow into the woods. Behind us the B. & L. E. drag puffs on toward Cleveland's main yard.

Our forces combined, Bessemer and Lackawanna approach the fire and kneel before the flames as if it is we who first established this jungle. The 'boes gathered there accept our arrival in silence, their talking and smoking and eating and drinking interrupted.

"Deirdey!"

A boy with a bright-blue kerchief about his throat leaps from the darkness where the light of the flames does not reach. He dashes across the open ground, skirting the fire, and throws himself into Deirdre's arms.

Deirdre catches him in midair and falls back—her laughter mixed with sobs.

III

Deirdre

10

Herbie squirms in my arms, kissing my cheeks and chin and mouth, my own arms squeezing his head and shoulders.

"Deirdey, I miss you."

Before he can say more he is pulled from my arms, and oh, I feel empty.

The big 'bo has acted so fast that everyone—the other 'boes at the fire, Bessemer, Lackawanna—all remain as we were, and I find my own arms wrapping the space that was Herbie's body.

With three strides the big 'bo, carrying my shrieking brother, crosses the open ground. He would disappear into the darkness, but one of the other 'boes, who's been shoving logs into the fire, throws a stick of wood between his feet, and the big 'bo falls forward. Slezak, as if he's been catapulted, is on him.

As Herbie squirts out of the 'bo's arms like a fumbled football, Lackawanna and Bessemer swarm over the man, kicking, punching, scratching. First on him, I'm first thrown, landing on someone's cardboard shelter. I grab a log and leap around to wait for an opportunity to swing. But Herbie runs to me and clutches my legs. He tries to reach my arms, the log, my hands, shouting all the while, his words obscured by his sobs as well as by the screams and curses pouring out of the eight savage kids and the 'bo, who, he must realize, is fighting for his life.

Like pieces of clothing being discarded, one or another of the kids flies free, but those who remain fight harder. Loose and one of the other Bessemer kids are hurled aside as the big 'bo stands erect. Slezak, growling, hangs on, chewing at the big 'bo's neck like an enraged beast seeking to find and tear the jugular vein. The remaining three Bessemer kids, on their knees at the 'bo's legs, try to butt him in the groin, but they can gain no leverage in the loose snow. Finally Slezak is shaken free, to sail through the air into the snow-heavy bushes. Scooping Herbie up in his arms, the 'bo dashes out of the firelight and into the woods.

Exhausted, stunned at the speed with which events have moved and stunned at my loss once again, I watch while the darkness swallows my little brother. I've held Herbie in my arms, I've felt his breath on my cheeks, I've heard his voice: "Deirdey, I miss you." I've saved him and lost him.

Someone produces a tin cup filled with coffee, someone else a slice of bread smeared with a substance sweet and sticky. Nursing our wounds, we regroup around the fire. So sore I can hardly move, I stare into the flames, as if they alone have the answers.

"Where will he take him? Did you hear him? He said, 'Deirdey.' " I speak to no one in particular.

"The 'bo has to hide."

The speaker, a man whose hair is so thick and ragged, he might be wearing a coonskin cap, is the one who tripped the big 'bo with the log.

"Hide where?"

"He's got places. . . ."

"Do you know him?" Willy asks. Willy's eyes are cut and swollen. One of them will surely be closed soon. Dear Willy.

Slezak has hurt his fist, is nursing it with the good hand. His face and neck, torn by a branch, are raw and bloody.

"We'll get him," Slezak says. "The next time . . ." and he leaves the threat hanging in the air.

"Do you know him?" Willy asks again.

"I know him," the 'bo replies. "I knew him early on. He was different then."

"Hell's bells, Red," a 'bo calls, "we was all different then."

"I want to keep after him," I say. "Right now. But I can't move. Every bone hurts. I can't walk. My ankle—"

"Take your time, sis," Red advises me. "He ain't goin' far, and a man that size leaves a trail. Like an elephant. Why do you want to tangle with him? Whadda you got against him? Take my advice, stay out of his path."

Willy stops holding chunks of packed snow on his eyes and peers across the fire at the 'bo called Red.

"Are you Rhode Island Red?"

"That's me."

"Dixie told us to look you up."

"Well, now, ain't that somethin'? You kids know Dixie?"

"We met him by the rails. He fed us. He's going nonstop to California."

Red laughs. "Dixie's been goin' nonstop to California for the last five years."

A few of the 'boes, unconcerned, turn in, wrapping themselves in rags other than those already being worn. A few use up the remains of the coffee and sit, bleary-eyed and fatigued, observing the flames. Loose and the others from Bessemer huddle together, like dogs licking their wounds. She urges me to figure out how we'll handle the big 'bo the next time.

"If there is a next time," an emaciated old 'bo warns us. "I was him, I'd just hightail it west, nonstop, like Dixie."

"Who's the kid?" Red asks.

"The kid?"

"That kid he had."

"My brother. He kidnaped him, dragged him off."

"But . . ." and Red catches himself.

"But what?" I ask, knowing I should not. I don't need to have clarified the shadow of the thought hovering at the back of my mind.

"He tried—leastwise it seems that way to me—he tried to stop you from fighting Big Oak."

I clutch Willy's wrist. Finally. We have a clue. An identity. "Is that his name? Big Oak?"

Rhode Island Red glances about, uneasy, as if he's betrayed a friend and will be denounced should his betrayal be recognized by any of the 'boes who've heard. But those who have not yet fallen asleep are not interested in the conversation between Rhode Island Red and these kids who have disturbed the nightly ritual of talk and smoke and drink.

"That's his name," Red says in a guarded whisper. "He'll head for California, right enough, but he won't be goin' nonstop like Dixie. Every drag will be swarmin' with bulls just praying to catch him."

With that Rhode Island Red finds more logs, settles them in the flames, and turns his back on me as if he's talked himself out or used up all his information. He expels his collection of snores and grunts.

When I begin to shiver, Loose prods and pushes me closer to the fire.

"We gotta go," I say. "We can't lose the trail now."

"I still have my knives," Slezak says. I think about that. I've used his knife once, out of fear. I returned it to him. Should I take it back? Can I use it again, this time out of hate? Slezak reaches inside his jacket and extends his arm, the thick black handle in his palm. His thumb and forefinger move and the blade leaps free of the wooden grip, its evil gleam flickering in the firelight. A minute, perhaps two minutes pass before I shake my head and look away. I can't take the thing into my hands. Slezak shrugs and returns the knife to its hiding place.

The many bodies of Lackawanna and Bessemer close on each other, to wrap themselves in each other's arms and legs, each other's coats and jackets. I can't help it—I don't want to, but I also fall asleep.

I waken to see Willy's face close to my own.

"He's up." Willy's voice is hushed.

Rhode Island Red is sitting at the fire, blankets and coats thrown over his shaggy head. From beneath the hood of ragged cloth his eyes are fixed on me. All the others—the adults and kids—are sleeping. The wind carries the noise of a passing freight, the call of the engine. It is that noise, perhaps, that has stirred Rhode Island Red, that has broken into his dreams. Has his need to say what he is about to say refused to let him sleep?

"Big Oak's his monicker," Red murmurs from beneath his hood. "He's the biggest, strongest damn man I ever did see. Lately he's mean, but used to be anyone could walk up to him and put him down, even punch him. He'd never fight back. Lately, well, 'boes stay away from him. That punk, the one he grabbed—"

"He's no punk. He's my brother."

"I didn't mean nothin', sister. A kid, he's with a jocker, that's what everyone calls him, a punk. But all the years I know Big Oak, he's never showed signs.

A 'bo can do what he wants, that's the rule of the road, sis, but I think an old 'bo like Big Oak takin' a young punk, well, I don't go for that."

"He's not a punk."

"O.K., O.K." Red moves forward to deposit more wood on the fire. As he rearranges the hood, his eyes gauge the other 'boes, all of whom are still asleep, or so given to their own sorrows that they pay no attention to the murmurs passing between Red and me. " 'Boes usually don't spout off like I do. But I don't like it, what he's doin'. He just ain't the man he used to be."

"If you were to guess where he's like to go now," Willy asks, "where would you guess?"

Red's hands fumble about beneath the rags and appear in his lap, holding a sack of Bull Durham and a cigarette paper. His body remains rigid. As if unattached, only the fingers move, folding and working until the paper is filled with tobacco and packed and rolled and moistened, and ready for smoking. After the match flares, a large cloud of smoke floats in the frozen air, seems to freeze itself and shatter.

"Chi."

"Chi?"

"Chicago."

"Where in Chicago? What street?"

"I don't know. That's where he's from."

"If the bulls are looking for him—"

"He'll take to the highway. Or walk. Some 'boes never hop drags—they feel safer hitchin' trucks or cars. Specially in good weather. But even weather like this there's drivers'll pick up 'boes. Father and son, that's what some driver'll think. He'll take pity and pick them up."

"Once we're in Chicago . . ."

Red shakes his head at Willy. "You gotta get there first. Tomorrow mornin', six-sixteen, at the water tower, the Western Express stops for ten minutes. Stay away from the tower; go a mile or so west, wait in the brush 'longside the tracks. You can hop it then. In Chi, well, get outa the yards as fast as you can." Rhode Island Red gazes about the jungle again to be sure none of this is being overheard.

"Sooner or later Big Oak'll appear at Ben Reitman's College of Hoboes on South Halsted. Or at Mother Greenstein's. Ask any 'bo or bull for directions. You'll catch him there sooner or later. What you do once you got him I don't know."

"We'll figure it out," I say. "This time Herbie won't get away."

The cigarette, given one last puff, is pulled backward into Red's mouth and is followed by sounds like those that accompany a cow's chewing its cud.

"It was summer," Red goes on, "I'd hang 'round

Grant Park. In the summer 'boes lie there on the grass and—"

"But it's not summer," Willy says, his voice edged with irritation.

"The main stem, then. West Madison, a place called the Workingman's Palace. 'Boes come there from all over the country for a meal. Might be news there. Farther down Madison at the Fremont Hotel, or Hogan's Flop. South of the main stem there's South State, called the Bums' Broadway. Burleycue joints and bookies and beer joints. Women on every corner. You got twenty-five cents, any one of those women will give you any information you want. If she ain't got it, she'll get it for another twenty-five cents."

With that, Rhode Island Red flops back into his rags and begins snoring.

"What do you think, Willy?"

The snoring stops. The rags speak, a jumble of words.

I lean forward to hear better.

"Did you say something, Red?"

"He's got a sister in Chi. Never did know her name. It was me, I'd track *her* down. He needs a place to hide. It was me, I'd go to my sister's."

For a time, after Rhode Island Red renews his snoring, Willy and I remain silent. I try to speak, but the words catch in my throat. We have information. We are no longer floundering.

"You awake?" Willy whispers.

"Yeah." I move my arm just enough to provide a sleeve for my nose. "You?"

"Yeah. What are you thinking?"

"It's . . . it's Christmas Eve, Willy. I'm thinking about Herbie."

Bessemer walks us to the tracks and wishes us luck. I thank them. Loose and Slezak compliment each other. Loose feels Slezak's arm under the wrappings of sleeves.

"You oughta be a boxer, you know that?"

Slezak all but squirms under the flattery.

"I ain't kiddin'. I've been around boxers all my life. My two brothers are boxers. If women were allowed to box, I'd be a boxer. You're good. I can tell."

Norman puts up his fists, pretending to challenge Slezak.

"Aw," he says, weaving and dodging, "I whi-whip him every d-day and twice on Su-Sundays. Right, S-Sleze?"

Still blushing, Slezak permits himself to be pushed and prodded by Norman. He even goes so far as to wince and plead for mercy.

"He'll n-never be able to g-get his h-hat on his h-head now. M-maybe I'll j-just have to take him d-down a size or t-two."

Slezak, laughing, taps Norman on the chin, and Norman pretends to stagger, then falls over.

Bessemer, finally leaving the tracks, goes down the hill, down a narrow road that has not been plowed, that leads into deeper snow. They turn and wave before they disappear.

The railroad bull seems to drop out of the sky.

"You kids are plannin' to hop the six-sixteen, right?"

"No, no. We're—"

"Sure, sure. You're out for the Easter parade."

He keeps the leather strap of his club wrapped around his wrist. The club flips, is caught, flips again. The bull looks fierce. But then the threat in his voice, in his appearance, softens. As if the holiday spirit had reached out to trap him.

"O.K., where you headed? Chi?"

"That's right," I say.

"Ah, you're goin' west to California, like all the other 'boes. Well, I wish I could. O.K., keep goin'. Promise you won't come back here, and I'll set you up a schedule. Understood?"

Slezak, reacting to the bull's authority, starts to

tell him we don't need his help. We're going to Chicago no matter what. But I cut in. "Sure," I say, "we understand." Let him perform his role, I decide.

"O.K. Out of Chicago take the Ninety-one Rock Island. Ten A.M. Hits Kansas City eleven the next morning. Five P.M. the next day, third day, it's in Tucumcari, New Mexico. Eight-thirty A.M. the fourth day, it's in El Paso, Texas. Seventh day, three P.M., you get into Los Angeles. Or take the old Ninety-one out of K.C. That becomes the Ute when it connects with the Denver and Rio Grande Western, in Denver. Pops over the Rockies into Salt Lake. From there you go Western Pacific into San Francisco. Remember now, I'm doin' you a favor. You ain't comin' back here."

"We promise. Honest."

"O.K. Just remember, cars are classified and fixed in the order they'll be detrained. San Francisco, for instance, should be coupled behind the engine. Cars for Kansas City, the first drop, would be coupled at the rear."

"Thank you, mister." My voice is sweeter than an angel's.

"Yeah," Norman adds, "thanks, m-m-mister."

The bull almost smiles. "M-M-Merry Christmas. Now g-g-get the hell outa here."

* * *

"Hey," Slezak says. "Looks like a hobo convention."

Every boxcar that has an open door is filled with hoboes. A few hardy or flamboyant men cling to the ladders or even stretch out on the decks. The blind is packed. Has every railroader made a secret holiday pact to permit one free ride?

"They're on their way to California," Willy says. "Most of them. They've had it with snow and ice."

"Ice," Norman says. "Boy, I'd like to go to C-California." Norman's voice is husky and his nose is stuffed.

"The last cars won't be so packed," Willy says, "if they're going to be dropped first."

His prediction proves correct, though even those cars have a significant contingent of 'boes. Four or five, who might be no older than fifteen, are crowded together in one corner, as if agreed to protect each other.

"Come on," a fat hobo shouts, "a couple you geezers give me a hand with this door."

Several men, laughing, give him a hand, then return to their places. Nobody has spoken the word aloud, but we know that it is Christmas. Today is Christmas Day. Perhaps because it is Christmas, perhaps because there are several bottles of wine traveling about the car, perhaps because there is plenty of tobacco and, after bags and boxes and pockets are emptied, there are varieties of food—whatever the reason, a spirit of festivity, of cheer, springs alive in the car.

The freight speeds across the countryside through the cold wind and the falling snow, but inside this car Christmas is being recognized and honored.

It proves to be more than Christmas. It is a picnic, a high school cookout at the beach, a Boy Scout jamboree, all of them here this wintry day to celebrate the birth of the Christ child. The 'bo who demanded help to close the sliding door turns out to be a triple-chinned woman in her sixties, perhaps her seventies. She has five children in tow, all of them eleven or twelve years old. She found them, she announces, in a stock car, where they'd settled to get warm. They'd been locked in by an unsuspecting checker. Queen Bee Pollard, as she is called by the 'boes, greets everyone with a "How-dee!" and a strong hug. She seems to know most of the older men.

All the passengers produce what they have. Those who have nothing to offer have to give, as Queen Bee shouts, exactly that: nothing. They are as welcome to share as anyone else. There are bags of coffee, several loaves of bread, sticks of moldy salami, cans of soup, vegetables limp or dry and usable if there were water, if there were pots, if there were a fire. There is no water, no pots, no fire. No matter. Food is meant to be eaten.

A harmonica, several harmonicas, appear. And a guitar. The songs are rowdy at first, but as the kids in the car begin to participate, the songs change. Like birds calling messages to each other just before a storm, the chirping, high-pitched voices dart through the car until the cynical and sullen older men give way.

Lackawanna is indistinguishable in the darkness from other gangs or individuals. All bulge with layers of sweaters and jackets and trousers. There are enough cigarettes always aglow, enough matches always being struck, to hold at bay the darkness inside the car. As cigarettes move from those who have something to those who have nothing, single faces pop into existence for a moment, hover, and then disappear. Songs surrender to stories, claims are shouted. Awe or disbelief or praise accompanies the glows or the flames.

The drag rumbles on, engine calling at the crossings, wind whistling through the narrow opening in the doorway. The man with the guitar picks out a chord, another. A harmonica joins the guitar. One and then another older 'bo contributes a song.

Everyone seems to know the words to one or two of the songs. If they don't, they pretend to know them. Now and then a 'bo, sometimes two or three, stands and attempts a jig or a two-step, but usually they are too drunk or too awkward or both, and they end up stretched along the ground or in the laps of friends. There seem to be no enemies this day.

Someone, shouting, "Merry Christmas," breaks the spell. Or creates a new one. After a short silence our voices, my voice and Willy's and then Slezak's and Norman's, rise above the hum of the wind, the drum of iron wheels on iron tracks.

> Silent night, holy night,
> All is calm, all is bright . . .

The 'boes who've been sleeping awaken. More cigarettes glow, more matches flare. Queen Bee's children join in. The voices of the children rise clear and pure and beautiful, voices of dirty, hungry, exhausted angels.

> O little town of Bethlehem,
> How still we see thee lie . . .

The voices of the children throw back the darkness, hang in the air like starlight.

> Oh come, all ye faithful,
> Joyful and triumphant . . .

The other 'boes join us. No harmonica now, or guitar. Only voices.

It came upon a midnight clear,
That glorious song of old . . .

No one can say who started it, but at one point there are a few matches flaming, then more, then matches bloom throughout the car. I cannot stop the tears from seeping between my closed eyelids and down my cheeks.

From angels bending near the earth
To touch their harps of gold.

Peace on the Earth, goodwill toward men . . .

11

South Bend. I point to a boxcar. "Look. The only open car in the whole line. Look where it's from."

In script, on the side: *Delaware, Lackawanna and Western.*

Norman jumps up and down. The excitement seems to clear his stuffed nose just enough to let him breathe well.

"Chesapeake, Delaware, Lackawanna," he sings. "Oh, where you worka, J-John? On the Delaware, L-L-Lackawan'. And whatta you worka, J-J-John?"

Slezak joins him. "I pooshada pooshada poosh."

Willy points to the sun that has just broken through.

"Hey, it's gonna be a sunny day."

He's right. The sun remains and the wind dies, so that by the time we catch a drag west, by the time we hit the main stem in Chicago, the crust on the snow is beginning to melt.

Norman gives Slezak an affectionate push. "It's s-sprig. Da b-boid is od da wig. Why, d-dat's absoid. I t-tawt da wig was od da b-boid."

We hit the main stem, West Madison, at noon, and the Presbyterian mission a few minutes later, to down a bowl of soup and two slices of bread that are almost fresh. Along with a rare treat, of which none of us takes more than two bites: a candy bar. Such a delicacy has to be preserved. We put in required hymn and prayer time to guarantee the night's food and flop. In five days, we're told, the mission will be having its New Year's Eve prayer and supper session. Being so young and so far from home, we're invited.

Outside, in the almost springtime warmth, we get directions from knowledgeable 'boes and make our plans. I'm reminded I have the final word regarding each of the separate missions.

First, on Willy's suggestion, Norman distributes two dollars to each of us, including himself.

"Dow," Norman says, after he distributes the money, "we got sebed d-dollars and sebed cedts left."

His nose is so stuffed he can hardly breathe.

Willy is to go out to Seventh and State Streets to Mother Greenstein's Restaurant, to collect information. Slezak is to cruise the Bums' Broadway. I'm to visit an old 'bo, Ben Reitman, who, a sympathetic cop tells me, "Admires every 'bo who can read and teaches every one who can't." Norman is to scout Bughouse Square and the Workingman's Palace and the flops around the Fremont Hotel.

If Rhode Island Red's advice is correct, we should have, by the end of the day, more information about Big Oak. Before we separate, I suggest we find a cheapo cafe and treat ourselves to real coffee and real doughnuts.

We walk along Madison, savoring the sights and sounds and smells of a city.

"If I close my eyes," Slezak says, "it's almost New York. I wish I *was* in New York."

"Sleze, dod't c-close your eyes. Sood as s-sprig c-comes, I w-wadda g-go hobe. B-baybe I cad f-fide by b-bother. I w-wadda go *hobe.* H-h-hobe!"

I can't believe they're all so nostalgic.

"Spring? Spring's months away. We're gonna find Herbie and be home in two weeks. I've got a feeling. Look, God's on our side. He's made it warm for us."

Indeed, the temperature is up to sixty degrees. Every 'bo on the street has removed at least one layer of garments to soak up the rare sunshine. Beyond Racine, missions lean on missions, shabby hotels meet shabbier hotels, sleazy bars spill out fumes of beer and sawdust, hoboes or tramps or bums evade recruiters from the Salvation Army. Shysters or crooks or thieves, prostitutes or hopheads or pushers, jackrollers or soap boxers or fortune tellers: the warm weather has brought them all into the streets.

"Let's go," I say. "Everybody meet back at the mission at four." I race off through the crowds, all of whom must think I've picked up something of value and am trying to escape. From the sidewalks as well as the street they cheer me on.

Four o'clock. The Presbyterian mission.

I arrive first. A few minutes later Slezak arrives, and ten minutes after that Willy appears. I can hardly restrain myself; I want to know everything immediately, but we've agreed that we'll wait until everyone returns before sharing our experiences. I pace back and forth in the fading sunlight.

"Let's just each of us say yes or no, we have news."

"Yes," Willy says.

Slezak nods. "Yes."

I know my face is beaming. "Me too, yes. Let's just say yes or no, is the news good? O.K.? Come on."

Willy grins. "Yes, yes, yes."

Slezak holds up his right fist and shakes it twice. "Yes, yes."

I'm delighted. And impatient. "Yes for me, too."

I try to be calm and silent in the mission's alcove, but I just can't wait any longer.

"Let's tell what we've got. When Norman gets here, if he's got good news, it'll make things even better. If he's got bad news or no news, well, it won't matter. O.K.?"

Slezak wants to wait for Norman, but Willy agrees with me. My optimism has infected him. Who should go first?

I scurry through the dining room and into the kitchen and return with three broom straws of different lengths. "Shortest goes first."

"Me," Slezak says as we compare our straws. "I'm first."

Slezak.

Yeah, I got some news. I'm walking along and I keep thinking, hey, I'm from New York. I've been around. You don't grow up in New York City, in the Bronx, and come out a rube. You know? But Bums' Broadway—whew! Those women, I wonder what they get paid, if they do get paid. 'Cause all I saw was down-and-outers. Those 'boes huffing and puffing down the street, most of them didn't have a penny for a cig.

I went to a couple women and they told me to shove off. They thought I was after what they were selling. I just wanted information, I said, and I flashed my money. Had the bills rolled up so they looked like I got maybe two, three times what I really got. Those dames ain't seen more'n a quarter at a time for years. Anyway, now they're willing to talk to me. I gave five of them the description of the big 'bo. None of them knew anything about the guy. I went into the penny arcades. 'Boes were just standing around. No pennies. No one knew anything about the 'bo. Then I meet this bookie. I tease him along, flash the bills. He doesn't know anything, but he's got a friend, a cop, and there's nothing this cop can't find out. Do I got a buck? Yeah, I got a buck, but only if the news I get's worth a buck. He says he'll be back, we should meet at Shorty's, a cafe, in half an hour. I can't do much else. I've tried everything and it didn't work, so I wait.

I walk around in the sun, asking 'boes about Big Oak and Herbie, but there's nothing. I mean nothing. I go to Shorty's at three. He's there, the bookie. He tells me this Big Oak goes to a place on Clark Street sometimes when he's in town. Place called the Blue Fish. People there, he says, are blowed-in-the-glass stiffs, sort of upper-crust down on their luck, but if there's ever prosperity again they'll be right back in their mansions. 'Boes there used to be doctors or lawyers or businessmen. I go there, find this 'bo used to be a banker in Indianapolis. People are talking politics. History and books and stuff like that. I find a friend of Big Oak's working there at the Blue Fish. This friend gets food for him when he's in town. Big Oak goes there, this friend says, to listen to arguments about politics and books. Now—you ready for this?—Big Oak was there yesterday. He was at the Blue Fish last night. Alone.

I was getting cold again, so I decide to come on back to the mission. No, no one, the friend, no one, knew if he was still in town or not.

That's it, that's all I got. Wait. Another thing. This friend gave Big Oak a bag of sandwiches. Peanut butter sandwiches. Ol' Herbie loves peanut butter. Remember? In the basement in New York? 'This finger next to your thumb. Scoop it out around the edge with your finger.' Deirdre, hey Deirdre, I'm sorry. I didn't mean . . . Where's Norman?

Willy.

This woman, Mother Greenstein, she's got a sign in front of her place. "Mother's Restaurant. Don't go hungry. See Mother." She's something. A couple antiques, they tell me Mother Greenstein hands out better food free than you'd get at the Blackstone or the Drake—those are fancy hotels—for pay. These two guys, they've been rich, traveled all over the country, the best hotels and restaurants, and they rave about Mother Greenstein's food. No one goes away from Mother Greenstein's hungry. If they have something to pay, they pay; if they don't, they get it free. She even gets people work sometimes, if they want work. She's got contacts uptown, even gets sick 'boes into clinics. Every Thanksgiving she throws a free supper. Calls it "The Feast of the Outcasts." 'Boes come from all over the city.

I talk to her. She asks me am I warm, do I have good shoes. I tell her yeah, but I got a sister, she's fourteen, she needs new shoes. Here you are, Deirdre. They ain't exactly new, and I got them big, but they're better than the ones you had before you got your high tops from that woman. The high tops ain't gonna last all your life.

So I describe Big Oak to Mother Greenstein. She knows him. Right off. Yeah, she knows him a long time. He's been coming around since the Depression started, since right after the Crash. Sometimes, especially the summer, he's there two, three times a week. His name—yep, we finally got a name—his name's Ketchell. She said he wanted to fight the Kaiser in the war, but the army wouldn't take him. They said their cots and their uniforms wouldn't fit him. Everything would have to be special made.

Well, when Lena Greenstein—that's her name—when she hears my story—and I tell her everything—she goes to a phone, and sure enough the operator gives her the names of seven Ketchell's. She writes down the numbers and calls each one. Pretends she's from the employment office and she's got a job for this man Ketchell and was this the right address? The Ketchell she's talking about is maybe thirty-five and he's big. The job she's got for him is for a big strong man. So is this Ketchell? Well, the sixth call's the one. "That's Thomas," the woman on the other end says. Mother Greenstein asks is Thomas home and what's his address?

The woman on the phone—she's Big Oak's, Thomas Ketchell's, sister. He's not home, but he will be soon. How soon? Tomorrow. He always comes home New Year's Eve, every year. New Year's Eve's got special memories for him. He never misses. So he'll be home tomorrow night.

But then she says something—Mother Greenstein tells me later. She says he's changed a lot. He used to be happy, but last time she saw him, about four months ago, he never laughs anymore. He was nervous last time, even talked about killing himself. He's always been so gentle, like a great big baby. So if the agency can get him a job, they'd really be saving his life.

Well, there you are. This is Saturday, December 26th. If he comes home for New Year's Eve, he'll be there Thursday, New Year's Eve. I got the address. It's on Cottage Grove. About a ten-minute walk from the University.

See, Deirdre, I told you. We'll get him. We're really closing in.

Hey, it's almost suppertime. I bet Norman got lost. We better glom some food and hold it for him. He'll be sore if we get to eat and he can't. I got this big sandwich. Mother Greenstein made it. Salami, corned beef, pickle, everything. If I hadn't eaten so much when I was there, I'd have eaten it already.

Tell you what. If Norman gets here in twenty minutes, he gets the whole sandwich. If he's later than twenty minutes, we share it. Right? I hope he's late.

Deirdre.

Well, this guy, Ben Reitman, he was a hobo for a long time, way back in 1910, even. He went to college and became a doctor. A real doctor. You ought to see the place he set up. A big hall like an auditorium. About two hundred people can sit in it. They have benches 'stead of chairs so 'boes hearing lectures don't fall asleep. Yeah, they have lectures, just like in a real college. In his office there are shelves from the floor to the ceiling, on every wall, and the shelves are filled with books. I couldn't read their names. They were words this long. He kept telling me I ought to go home. Home was better than being a hobo, especially for kids, no matter how tough it was at home. And stay away from jungles, he said. They're bad places for girls.

Anyway, at this college all the teachers—he calls them professors—they're hoboes. They teach all kinds of things. Students are all 'boes. Sometimes professors from the real University come over. Students, too, sometimes.

I asked Reitman if he knows Big Oak. He does. Big Oak has been at the college several times. Especially summer and fall. He's smart, Reitman says. Once he got into an argument with a professor from the real college about children and the Depression. I got chills when Reitman told me this, so I told him why I'm trying to track down Big Oak. He couldn't believe it. It must be a different 'bo. I said it was the same guy. Hadn't Big Oak talked about children? Wasn't that enough to convince Reitman?

Reitman said yeah, he'd talked about children, with this psy— I forget the word. He's a head doctor. Big

Oak, he was all tore up about what the Depression's done to children.

I gave up and left. So yeah, like both of you, I found out he's from around here, and yeah, he'll probably come to one of the classes at Reitman's college, and when he does Reitman will talk to him. Reitman didn't know where he lived, but he said he'd get the address and give it to me. But Willy, you got it. You and Slezak both really discovered important facts.

New Year's Eve we'll be ready. We've got to talk, got to plan. This time we'll be ready.

Hey, where's Norman?

The day's warmth is gone. The rising wind chills the evening. When Norman does not show up for supper, and doesn't show up when we get our cot notices, we decide he must have run into a good bed-and-table and is making the best of it. I'm worried. I want to go look for him. So does Willy and Slezak. But now it's snowing hard and the temperature has dropped below freezing. Slezak, who's never bothered by cold, says he can get to Hogan's Flop, wherever it is, where Norman was supposed to go, without us. Willy tells him to wait, and he goes to the woman who's in charge of Sally's. Sister Martha. She calls the police. In weather like this, she tells Slezak, he better stay where he is. Slezak tries to argue, but she says if this was his hometown, O.K., but this is Chicago.

The cops ask us questions—what Norman looks like, where he might be, and if they find him where should they take him. Sister Martha insists they bring him right here. He'll need hot soup more than anything else.

None of us—Willy or Slezak or me—none of us sleeps while we wait. About midnight Sister Martha tells us the police called. They haven't found him. They'll keep looking. He probably went in somewhere to get out of the cold.

When Norman doesn't appear for bread and coffee at breakfast time, we bundle up in our rags and wrap our feet. It is cold. With scarves protecting throats and faces, we find our way down the stem to Hogan's Flop, one of the places Norman was going to investigate.

The sunshine and warmth of yesterday are not even memories. The snow crunches under our feet as we walk, and our breath is almost solid in the air.

We have to ask several 'boes where Hogan's Flop is located, and when standing directly in front of it, I have to ask another 'bo how to get in. The 'bo points out the almost invisible narrow stairway.

At the top of the stairs, after I knock, the door

squeaks open. One bulb hangs from the ceiling at the inside entryway. No, the clerk says, he can't remember a little 'bo who fits the description I give him. Yeah, sure, we can look around.

Inside are thirty or forty men sleeping on the floor. A few have paper under their bodies, between their bones and the boards. Someone is always snoring or spitting or coughing. Norman is not among them.

An old man, using a broom as a cane, approaches the clerk and murmurs in his ear. The clerk calls me.

"Hey, you wanna come down here?" He pulls on his overcoat and fur hat and rabbit-skin gloves, and we follow him through the door and down the stairway. The wind is so bitter, the clerk covers his ears with his gloved hands.

Under the stairs, among the boxes and garbage cans, is a bundle of rags. The clerk grunts as he tries to pick them up. They are frozen to the ground. He and the old man and Slezak, using sticks found near the garbage cans, pry the bundle free and turn it over.

Norman's face is white crystal. His body, not much larger than a dog's, is frozen stiff. His left arm is up and out in what might be a salute or what might have been a last effort to grab something to pull himself from the freezing ground. Had he fallen? Had he simply succumbed to the freeze? He wasn't strong, he was frail in fact. He'd had a bad cold, he was malnourished. Had he fallen and crawled and, as freezing people often do, just given in to the desire, almost the main desire in his life, to sleep?

Oh my dear Norman, I will remember you and love you forever.

12

Mother Greenstein arranges the burial for the morning of New Year's Eve day. She knows people who know certain Jewish philanthropists who will pay for a plot in a Jewish cemetery.

A friend of Mother Greenstein's has purchased clean clothing for the three of us, the three last members of Lackawanna. We are permitted to use her bathroom only if we agree to soak our heads and bodies in a bug-killing lotion that smells of sulphur. We've got to be clean. Our clothes, even the clothes I got at the Kellars' house in Cleveland, are stuffed into a bag and burned in the furnace. A cheap and practical delousing technique.

Standing at the side of the coffin, I cannot believe that the oversize doll lying on the pale-blue satin can be Norman. His rags have been replaced by a new dark suit, and his long hair has been trimmed and combed. Spots of rouge ride high on the cheeks of his polished face. His arms are close against the sides of his body, the hands long and delicate and white. Dirt has been cleaned from under his fingernails.

As the friends Mother Greenstein has collected to pray, and the rabbi, sing a strange melody in a strange language, I offer Norman a silent promise.

"When we get back to New York, I'll find your mother. I promise you, Norman. No matter how long it takes."

Bathed and in our new clothes, we ride to the cemetery in a large black Studebaker. About fifteen mourners, recruited from Jewish families in the city, stand in for Norman's family. There are lots of prayers and tears and sympathy for the deceased orphan.

In an ankle-length woolen skirt and a black tufted coat lent me for the occasion, I keep shifting my thoughts from the mounds of frozen muck above the hole in the ground to Herbie being hauled from the firelight into the darkness to my own inactivity now, while Big Oak and Herbie move farther away from me. I should be chasing them, following them. Then the thud of frozen dirt falling on the coffin brings me back to the moment. I think of Norman's constant complaints about the cold. Now he himself is icy cold. Why didn't I ever thank him? Why didn't I tell him I'd be forever grateful? How will I tell Herbie about Norman's death? Will he blame me? I weep for my shame as much as for my loss. Both of my losses.

When I raise my eyes, I see, across the banks of iced mud and the hole now being filled, Slezak and Willy staring down at the coffin, which is slowly disappearing beneath the muck. They lean against each other, shoulders touching, as if strength flows from one to the other, as if strength is all that is left to be shared. Slezak, the tough surly Slezak, who fears nothing and no one, is shaking his head, seemingly stunned, confused. Is he finally frightened? Why, I wonder, aren't we all at home? Why aren't we warm and well fed and at school, playing games, listening to music, dancing, going to the movies? What has happened to the world? Who has done this cruel thing to us? Will it ever be different? Someone must pay for this.

* * *

On our way back to the city in the Studebaker, Willy catches my hand, holds it, squeezes it. I am about to thank him and Slezak now, while I think about it—who can know what might happen tonight or tomorrow?—but Slezak, who has been brooding ever since we left the cemetery, says, "You know what I'm thinking?"

I wait, wishing he'd not spoken so I could have expressed my feelings as they swept over me.

Slezak wipes the steam from the window.

"That big sandwich. We held it for him. Then we ate it. You know, he didn't just die cold. He died hungry, too."

I remain silent.

Mother Greenstein takes pity on us. We can keep our new clothes, except my coat, which has to be returned to the young woman who owns it.

We are permitted to use Mother Greenstein's bathroom again before we leave. She hugs us as we stand at the door, ready to return to the hunt for Big Oak. She gives each of us a bundle containing long underwear and thick woolen sweaters and scarves. In addition, each of us, thanks to one of the still surviving clothing stores, has a new fingertip lumber jacket guaranteed to be impervious to wind, rain, or snow.

Mother Greenstein holds out a long white envelope.

"This is money the mortician found in Norman's clothing. Who should I give it to? Who's the leader?" Slezak and Willy point to me. I accept the envelope and place it in one of the red plaid pockets of my new lumber jacket.

On the trip back to the mission I open the envelope. I hold it out for Willy and Slezak to see. Inside are three ten-dollar bills.

We want to order a full meal, our first ever at a restaurant, but how can we? Norman would have wanted us to. I know that. But all we order is pie, two slices each, and coffee, with real cream, not milk. Even that goes down hard.

One of the waitresses thinks we're broke. She offers us sandwiches, free. We can't. I gag at the thought.

"What we ought to do," Slezak says, while shaking his head, indicating he couldn't do it, "we oughta order chocolate cake." He swallows hard. "In memory, you know."

We can't do it.

The waitresses are hanging balloons and crêpe paper from wall to wall, in preparation for the midnight party. They invite us to come back. Sure, Willy and Slezak say, they just might, but they know they won't. They have other plans.

I leave a quarter tip and then we hurry outside, into the cold, to take a streetcar to Cottage Grove Avenue.

During the ride there is a brief discussion about the tactics we've agreed on. None of us wants to appear especially excited because, as we've advised each other, the important thing now is to be calm and controlled. Though we do not mention the possibility, the probability, the certainty, that our long search is about to be ended, I know that Willy and Slezak too must be thinking of nothing else.

We reconnoiter the house at 5424 South Cottage Grove for several minutes after our arrival, and then we agree that both the front and the rear of the house must be guarded.

Slezak, the ever-ready Indian scout, makes several exploratory missions to windows and doors and returns to share his findings. Yes, there are people inside. Yes, there seems to be a party in progress, though it doesn't exactly look like a party. Everyone is quiet; no one seems especially happy.

The prospect of seeing Herbie, of rescuing him, adds to the warmth I find in my plaid jacket. Chin tucked down into the rolled collar and the wool scarf, I consider the emptiness in my own heart, or rather in my chest, where my heart should be. I have a sudden painful longing for Carl to be here, to participate in the ending. And Norman. Everyone should be here now.

Leaning against the tree, scarf concealing all but his eyes, Willy keeps constant watch up and down the sidewalk. If anyone appears, he will see them in time to conceal himself behind the thick trunk.

The outcome—if Big Oak does appear tonight—will be different from the one back at the jungle. We are ready for him tonight. We're united. I'm glad we agreed to rely on no one but ourselves, certainly not the police. Not now. We've rejected the police, not because the police might be insensitive or contemptuous, which they probably would be, but because the world, our world, my world, is no longer the place in which disinterested police and judges and juries make decisions regarding justice. Justice will be defined by the victims tonight.

I wait in front of the house, having already added to Mother Greenstein's clothing contribution other contributions from Sister Martha. I wear, over long underwear and under the wool skirt, two pairs of trousers. I rehearse in my mind the plans already discussed, almost choreographed. While Slezak and

Willy divert Big Oak, I'll grab Herbie and run. I've refused Slezak's offer of a knife. I don't want it. I could not use it if I had it. All I want is to rescue Herbie. I think about the intensity of Slezak's anger and how, at one time, I was frightened by just such anger. It was that, the violence, that drove Herbie and me out of our home.

Have I, I wonder, changed, as all the others have? Did anyone—our parents, our brothers or sisters, we ourselves—did anyone think that when Willy or Carl or Slezak or Norman, when any of us were fourteen or fifteen, we might be stumbling about in the railroad yards, on the streets, at soup lines, begging for food, pleading for a warm place to sleep? What will happen to me? To Herbie? After I escape with Herbie, after we return to New York, will Herbie be better off than he is now? Will he forget his torture?

I do not permit myself to think about the effects these weeks have had on Herbie. Nor do the others. As if by agreement, no one has talked about it. I have so strongly denied attention to it that not even my dreams will include it. We will forget it, that's all. We—Herbie and I—will put it out of our minds. I will not let myself be destroyed by despair, I will not let him be destroyed by guilt. That was what happened to my mother. Not me, not me! And not Herbie. We will be my father's golden angels again.

*   *   *

There had never been a hint, when my father had been alive, that my life would ever be anything but a life of love and joy. Golden angels he had called us both, me and Herbie. My older sister had never been considered an angel of any substance, gold or silver or iron. With our fair skin and our blue eyes and our red hair, Herbie and I had been smothered with love, with attention. But when my father began to change, when he lost his job and everyone else lost their jobs and he stood in line for Welfare handouts, when they had to limit the meals from three to two and then to ration the food, and then when he had to stay away from the house so there might be more food for me and Herbie, then the interior of the house and the exterior of him began changing at the same time. Color disappeared from walls and skin. That drab grayness of despair covered every object once vibrant and beloved. Sofa, chairs, windows, tables: gray, dusty, torn. My father's face, his hands, his eyes: gray, scaled, defeated.

The new man, the second father, the stepfather, had been angry and lost even before he entered our house, before he sought to set his stamp on the mother, on her daughters, on her son. She, the mother, gave up resisting, gave up caring, went for days, weeks, not touching us, not talking to us, not caring about the appearance of her house or her body. When she, too, began to share his bottles and she, too, began to silently accept his punches (on her as well as on her daughters as well as on her son), and when Herbie ran to me for protection, for love, I assumed the role of mother, of protector, without so much as a moment of doubt. The morning Herbie and I walked out of the house we wept, but our mother was laughing on the back porch with that new man.

Alert now beneath the tree in a strange and frozen city almost a thousand miles from home, or where home once was, I clench my fists as Slezak has taught me to clench them: fingers close together and pressing into the palm, thumb far forward and angled down so the fist is like a piece of iron, not a mere collection of skin and vulnerable bones. I want to strike out at something solid, something human, at the faces and voices that have converted me into a hater, a fury, a killer. Because *killer*, I know, is what I could easily be.

Now and then groups of students—at least they are young people—appear, to march up or down the street to one or another of the small homes. Music spills out of a large house across the street. A Model A Ford chugs past, horn honking. The young people inside the car are cheering, as if they're in a stadium urging their team on toward the goal line.

The Ford draws up to the curb, and the students leap out to race up the steps, still singing. From behind my tree I follow the car and its occupants with hungry eyes. So there actually are young people who are not starving, who probably have never been cold, who have never begged for pennies. Tonight these people, just two or three or four years older than I am, will be welcoming in the new year. Well, if all goes according to plan, I too will be celebrating. And so will Herbie.

I have been so preoccupied with the car and the young people, I do not hear the crunch of shoes on the snow until the man is almost at the tree. I hold my breath and press my body against the trunk. It must be that immobility, it must be the merging of body and tree into one dark shape, that keeps the man from seeing me. He walks past the tree and goes through the gate.

It is Big Oak, and he is alone.

13

Big Oak walks slowly, slightly bent, up the path that has been sprinkled with ashes. Up the steps and onto the porch. Soon after he knocks on the door, it is opened by a large, elderly woman. The two of them embrace, and she leads him into the house. The door closes behind them.

My hands, out of my pockets, are trembling. When I try to walk, my heavy feet refuse to do my bidding.

I find myself going through the gate, walking along the ash-covered path. But I am grabbed from behind and held.

"No," Willy whispers. "Remember our plan."

We return to the tree, and there on the sidewalk, on the packed snow, we debate our next move. Bells begin to chime at the University.

Slezak starts counting aloud. He says, when the chimes reach eleven and stop, "It's almost 1932."

"He's left Herbie somewhere. I'm sure of it."

Willy agrees. Neither of us dares consider the thought that pricks at our minds, the thought that Herbie might be dead.

"We can't jump him," I say. "Not till we know where he has Herbie. If he knows we're here, he'll never lead us to Herbie."

"We'll have to wait," Willy says. "When he leaves, we'll follow him."

"But what if he stays all night?" Slezak says. "He lives here."

I know that Slezak is thinking the same as I am, as Willy is. We are, again, seeing Norman's stiff body, his arm outstretched.

Slezak, the realist, can only say what he thinks.

"What if he doesn't have Herbie? What if Herbie escaped? What if he—well, what if he's killed Herbie?"

There it is, in the open. I leave the tree and step into the street. I can hear Willy arguing with Slezak, calling him stupid for having said it aloud. I listen to the sounds from the house, the students singing, the music, the cheer and hope and happiness. I turn back. The house that Big Oak entered is quiet, as if there is regret for the old year's ending.

I look directly at Slezak, shaking my head.

"He didn't kill Herbie. I know it, I just know it. He has Herbie hidden somewhere. If Herbie did escape, well, he's on his way back east. Either way, we can't know unless we wait and follow Big Oak."

Willy and Slezak agree. There is no other choice.

"I just hope he doesn't stay all night," Slezak says.

"If he does," I tell him, "so do we."

Then, thinking of Norman's death, I take Slezak's and Willy's hands in my own.

"I know you're both cold. And I know you're hungry. It seems we're always cold and hungry. I can't remember when I wasn't. But this isn't your fight. You've both helped me more than brothers or sisters would have. I want you as friends all my life—I don't ever want to lose you. Sometimes I catch myself thinking, when I grow up I'll marry one of you and have kids. But who wants kids cold and hungry like we've been? I'll never be able to thank you as much as I want to. But at least I've told you. I never had the chance to tell Norman. Why don't you both go back to the mission, where it's warm? Or to Mother Greenstein's? She'll take care—"

"We're staying," Willy says. "At least I am."

Slezak stomps his feet. "We're staying."

"O.K. Then we'll take turns. One watches while the other two sleep. That O.K.?"

Yes, that will be O.K. But where will we sleep? In the tree? And who'll take the first watch?

I insist on being first.

Slezak points across the street.

"That Ford. I bet those students stay at that party till late. We can sleep in the car. They probably even have blankets."

He's correct. There is not just one blanket, there are two. Curled together, arms around each other, with the two blankets tucked about them, Slezak and Willy sleep. For only a minute, it seems, before I shake them awake.

"He's going down the street," I whisper. "Come on."

A moment after Willy and Slezak fight free of their blankets and stumble out of the car to follow me, Slezak calls, "Wait."

He returns to the Ford, crawls inside, and reappears with the two blankets under his arm.

"Easy," I caution them when they catch up with me. "We don't want him to know we're after him."

Seeing the blankets, I have an idea.

"We'll pretend we're students. We can wrap up in the blankets, keep them over our heads. If he sees us, he'll think we're students. Let's sing."

"If Herbie . . ." but I don't end my sentence. If Herbie was here, we'd sing my father's songs.

"When I'm old enough," Willy says, "I'm going to college. I want to learn things. I want to be a doctor maybe. I want to help people."

Yes, you will be a helper of people, Willy.

"Watch him," Slezak whispers.

Big Oak turns from Cottage Grove and disappears down another street. There are no lamps here. But there is an almost fluorescent blue light distributed by the moon. We stop singing. That, I say, will make him think we've gone on. The dark figure moves ahead of us, visible against the snow. As we follow, silent now under the cold moonlight, we crowd close against walls and bushes. The walls and bushes give way to trees. The trees thin out and give way to an empty field deep with snow. Big Oak leaves the trees and disappears.

"I bet he went down a bank," Slezak says. "We'll see him again when he—There he is. We'll have to wait till he gets across the field. If we get on it now, he'll see us."

Willy is anxious. "We can't let him get too far ahead or we'll lose him."

Slezak, the great hunter, the crafty guide, offers us the benefit of his vast experience.

"Not in this snow. He can't shake us. We can track him."

Big Oak continues across the field, a lone figure in the polar whiteness. When he reaches the opposite end and disappears, we leave the protective shadows and advance to the bank. There are Big Oak's prints.

The snow on the field is so deep, we're exhausted before we're halfway across the field. But we continue, fearful that Big Oak might turn around for some reason and discover us.

"No talking now," Slezak says.

Head low, almost sniffing Big Oak's trail, Slezak leads us on across the field until we reach a collection of buildings that prove to be huge wooden storage sheds.

We all pause, then crouch, as yellow light flashes and flickers in one of the nearby sheds. The light finally settles into a shimmering gold glow behind a window.

Slezak, who has continued fighting his way through the snow, reaches the window first. By the time Willy and I join him, he is peering inside. He lowers his body and motions me to the window. Though I raise myself on tiptoes, my eyes do not reach above the lower sill. Willy and Slezak wrap their arms about my legs, just above the knees, and lift me.

There on the floor, sitting before a metal drum filled with flames, is Herbie. He's wrapped in blankets, and in front of him, spread on a newspaper, are plates of food and a cup of steaming coffee. There are two thermos bottles on the newspaper, one of them open and one of them corked. Herbie is eating. And laughing. When one of Big Oak's hands goes out to touch the top of his head, Herbie does not draw away. How can he possibly be unaware of that hand hovering above him?

Down on the snow again, kneeling, I wonder if I'll be able to straighten up, to stand. Every muscle is weak, quivering, threatening rebellion. I fight against the nausea that rises in my throat. Herbie is laughing, he's not sad, he's not even frightened. He is—no doubt about it—he is happy. He doesn't miss me at all. He looks like he'd be content to live without me for the rest of his life.

Something's wrong. He must be acting, he must be pretending.

I squat above the snow, struggling to make sense out of the thoughts that form and fade, that rush through my mind. Slezak and Willy, kneeling beside me, are waiting for my signal to put our plan into action. Willy nudges me, points toward the door. But a loud rich laugh inside the shed penetrates the wooden wall, the glass window, hovers in the air as if frozen into a solid mass, echoes and reechoes in my ears. Again, louder, richer.

I pivot in the snow to face Slezak and hold out my right hand, making a specific gesture with my fingers. Slezak, elated, grins and withdraws two knives from an inner pocket. He hands me the switchblade, keeping for himself the larger hunting knife. He reaches inside his clothing again and brings out a wide-bladed, black-handled Barlow knife, which, as agreed upon, he gives to Willy.

I stand, a new and intense resolve in my heart, in the way I move, almost in the way I breathe. I point to the door and motion for Slezak and Willy to follow me. After removing a glove and stuffing it into a pocket, I rap the door twice with my bare knuckles.

The firelight dims in the window. Silence. A long silence, then a voice rises from inside. Subdued. Suspicious.

"Who's there?"

Slezak raises his fist to pound the door, but I stop it as I hear footsteps inside.

The doorknob twists, the door opens, the opening widens. Big Oak waits inside the entry. The door opens wider, and he leans forward to peer into the darkness. The firelight behind him distorts the size and shape of his head, of his arms and legs, so that he looks like a giant insect.

Slezak, then Willy and I leap from the darkness.

When Big Oak falls back, trying to slam the door, something, the door or a bottle or his own enormous feet, something trips him. He starts to fall but struggles, arms and legs flailing to regain his balance so he won't be taken to the floor by his attackers.

Though the battle seems to go on for minutes, for hours, will never end, it is over in fifteen or twenty seconds.

Slezak, who has already begun the swing of his long knife, has no time when Big Oak falls to redirect his arm or reposition his body for a second effort. He is caught by one of Big Oak's flailing arms. The blow could not be more effective were it intentional. The huge fist, half the size of Slezak's head, strikes Slezak on the temple, and he falls to the floor as if he's been shot. The knife sails into the shadows.

Willy, grunting with the effort, has been stabbing with his Barlow knife, but the short blade will not penetrate Big Oak's coat. Willy, the next victim of the flailing arms, tumbles backward, flipflopping like a gymnast, to bounce off the wall and lie still near the doorway.

Finding my knife useless against the folds of cloth,

I reach for the unprotected throat. But all strength seems to have deserted me. My legs are so heavy, I cannot leap a second time. I scream, knowing that if I fail I might never have another chance. Big Oak will escape again. I will lose Herbie forever. I hear my own scream, but I also hear the screams of someone else. Not a man's voice, but a child's. It's Herbie. He is clutching my legs, trying to restrain my attack.

"Don't . . . please, Deirdey . . . stop. . . ."

Exhausted, confused, I do as he pleads. I stop. Big Oak is flat against a wall. He will not resist any longer. I know that. He stands there, gasping, his chin up, as if exposing his throat for my knife.

"Deirdey, don't hurt him. Please don't, Deirdey. I'll come with you if you don't hurt him."

My fingers lose their power to grip the knife. It drops to the floor.

"You promise, Deirdey? Do you promise? I'll come with you, but you gotta leave him alone."

"I promise."

Herbie, continuing to observe me as he crosses the room, reaches the big 'bo and gazes up into his face. Big Oak slides down along the wall to the floor, where he sits, as Herbie whispers into his ear. Big Oak nods, lowers his head into his arms. Astonished first, then humiliated, disgusted, almost angry, I watch Herbie hug the man.

Without so much as a glance toward me, toward Willy, who has finally managed to stand, toward Slezak, who is groaning and moving his arms, Big Oak rises. He glides past me with long, loping, almost graceful strides. He goes through the door without looking back.

Herbie, kneeling on a rug at the fire, is weeping. Sniffling, struggling to control his sobs, he wipes his nose along the sleeve of his right arm and turns his wet face up to me.

14

Within my arms, pressed against my body, Herbie moves his head so he can see around me, so he can observe Willy clinging to the wall and Slezak, sitting up, head in his arms, groaning.

Herbie pulls free. I remain on my knees, my fingers gripping my jacket, as I wait for the signal from Herbie that my attention, my love, will be welcomed again. But his eyes, in his pinched face, are almost opaque. He does not smile, he does not talk, he seems disinterested. When I stand, he stands too, but he remains mute, apparently without feeling, as I wrap his throat with scarves and button his various sweaters and jackets and draw the wool hat down over his ears. When I feel for his hand and lift it, and pull him toward the door, he does not resist. He sees Willy and Slezak, but is not interested in talking to them or even recognizing them. I lead him outside, past the sheds and onto the field of snow. Looking back, I see a figure emerge from the shed, then a second figure.

Big Oak's tracks and our tracks, made earlier, are dark blotches in the moonlit snow.

For the rest of the night and the following day—New Year's Day, the first day of January of the new year, 1932—the only reference to the struggle that occurred in the shed is a comment by Slezak that his head aches, his neck aches, his back and belly and bottom ache. The only part of him that does not ache is the little toe on his left foot.

Herbie remains in a dull-eyed apathy, an unyielding silence. He has little energy. With his ability to chase a fast drag diminished, Lackawanna has no choice but to hover at the fringes of the yards, where the cars have not been collected or cleared by inspectors.

In Cleveland, Ohio, at the junkyard, Bessemer welcomes us. Not with a loud celebration, but with a casual recognition that the mission has been accomplished. No questions are asked. Herbie is safe, as healthy as might be expected after such an ordeal. No need, I decide, to inform Loose or anyone else of the details. There is no comment about Norman's absence.

The silent Herbie, pale, with new dark shadows under his eyes, follows me wherever I go, close enough always to be able to touch me without extending his arm. He is indulged by everyone, not just me. Tough, loud, blustering Loose, concerned at Herbie's refusal to eat, cuts his wieners into bite-sized chunks and shapes his bread into dough images of mice or rabbits. She even offers to spoon-feed him, a gesture that all but shames him into accepting food.

At night Loose and I make two or three trips to the backseat of the Dodge where Herbie and I share a pile of coats and blankets. He does not even try to feign sleep but gazes at us with wide-open eyes.

On the third day—for no apparent reason—Herbie bursts into tears when I offer the rare delicacy of hot chocolate. Hot chocolate was once our mother's favorite drink. Loose wonders if I should take Herbie to a doctor.

"I'm taking him home," I say. "Maybe he'll be better when he's home."

"You mean his real home, your mom and dad's home?"

"No. I mean our home. Lackawanna's. If it's still there."

I think about her words. I've not really thought of it, but there is no more *mom and dad's home*. What will we do, Herbie and I? What will I do?

Early on a Tuesday morning Loose and two other members of Bessemer, all of them familiar with local yards and schedules, lead Lackawanna to the Columbus yards and guide us at the precise minute to the appropriate line of cars. Loose offers us $4.35 from their kitty. Willy, who has assumed Norman's role as treasurer, thanks her.

"We still have a couple bucks saved from Mother Greenstein."

Just before the drag starts moving, a half dozen other 'boes aboard the selected boxcar observe three kids hoisting a smaller kid into the car and then climbing in themselves. The three bigger kids stand at the open door and wave farewell to the kids below, who are kicking at the ankle-deep snow. In silence, huddled together, shivering, the 'boes watch the kids settle in a far corner. They watch the smallest boy clutching the hands of one of the others very tightly, as if he intends to keep the grip forever.

Once the drag picks up speed, two of the older 'boes stand and lean against the door and slide it closed, shutting out the falling snow, the crying wind, the fences and fields and small towns rushing by. Heading east, we're heading east, Herbie. We're going home.

A nurse informs us that Carl has been permitted freedom, but he is due back the following day for a final examination before being fully discharged. We'll find him in the Salvation Army mission.

Willy volunteers to approach the Sally director, a tall iron-jawed woman whose stiff black jacket and tight collar keep her trapped at constant military attention. Yes, there was a boy named Carl here. Yes, this Carl had his arm in a sling. At her recommendation, Sally has bent the rules a bit, permitting Carl to stay longer than the usual three-night limit. Are there enough cots for Carl's four friends tonight? Yes, but there can be no guarantee for tomorrow night.

Lackawanna registers and sits with a dozen other new recruits in a room that serves as a chapel. We sing our hymns, pretending to pay close attention to the leader's conversations with the Almighty.

Carl sneaks up behind us in the middle of the second stanza of "Onward, Christian Soldiers" and places one strong hand on Willy's shoulder and one weak hand on mine.

"So you made it. Hey, Herbie, how you doin'?"

Herbie almost smiles.

Carl pretends to punch the silent, brooding Slezak and the unusually reserved Willy. He glances about the room. He is about to ask about Norman but, anticipating the question, I shake my head.

Having received the message, Carl sits on a chair behind us, strangers on either side. When he sees my eyes fill with tears, he swallows hard and picks up the words of the hymn.

There are two reasons to be cautious now. Carl's shoulder is healing, but he will have to be careful for another month or two, and Herbie still moves as if he's about to drop off to sleep.

Following the pattern set by the rest of us, Carl asks Herbie nothing about his weeks with Big Oak. Like the others, he respects Herbie's inability, or unwillingness, to talk about his ordeal. All three of them seem to know, as if there has been a discussion and a mutual agreement, that by not talking about what has happened, Herbie will forget its reality. Or will not believe it when he does remember it. Should he be unable to forget, he will know at least that no one blames him, no one feels contempt for him, Herbie is still ours; we, Lackawanna, are still Herbie's.

"One for all and all for one."

"Hey," Carl says, "I got a new copy of *The Three*

Musketeers. Soon as we get settled down, I'll start reading it to you."

Herbie's interest seems promising.

The past invades and conquers my discipline once.

We are riding a drag on the New York Central. An old friend. Only Willy and I are awake.

Snow has been falling for three days, piling up drifts that have to be cleared by pushers and section gangs every three or four hours. The wind cannot be heard above the rumbling wheels, but it's there, adding to the sway of the car.

Groups of 'boes are gathered in the darkness, four different clusters of men and kids that reserve much of their energy by not bothering to talk, not bothering to move.

Lackawanna has shared nothing but a loaf of bread all day. Herbie, only his blue eyes visible within the wool bindings, seems unaffected by the cold, even unaffected by his hunger. I know better, and am worried. Herbie has lost weight, and his face, always pale, has taken on a gray pallor. For days he has remained unresponsive to embraces or voices or food. Slezak has shaken free of his humiliation, and Willy and Carl even crack jokes. No longer concerned about the responsibilities of leadership, Willy has become less serious. Occasionally, using a 39-card deck, he plays poker with Slezak; and after winning $44,000, he agrees to accept monthly payments of 87¢ until the debt's clear.

Out of nowhere, as if we have just been discussing the past weeks, I whisper, "Do you think he'll ever forget, Willy?"

Willy has had the warmth of Carl's body at his side.

"You and Slezak and Carl and I," Willy replies, "we'll never forget each other. We'll always remember how it's been since we got together at Hoover Valley. Ward, Momma, Poppa . . . I'll never forget them. Why should Herbie forget? How can he? Will you forget, Deirdre?"

I take a deep breath, sob once, and then give way to a weeping that seems to rise up from the base of my spine, a weeping so painful I cannot endure it alone. I reach for Willy, I try and fail to say his name. Willy takes me in his arms to comfort me even as I hold and comfort the sleeping Herbie. Or is he sleeping? Does he hear? Does he wonder?

There is a telephone on the wall outside the post office. Willy, his coins ready, deposits two dimes and a nickel when the operator requests them.

"Hello, this is Stevenson."

"Mr. Stevenson, this is Willy . . . William. You helped me find my little brother."

"I'll be doggoned. There you are. Where in blue blazes are you? Your sister with you?"

"Yes, she's with me. We're in New York. We're going . . . well, I guess we can call it home."

"Wait a minute. Did you just say I helped you find your little brother? You found him?"

"Yes. In Chicago."

"Well, by gum! It goes to show. His eye is on the sparrow. You gotta have faith. Is he O.K.?"

"He's O.K. Tired but O.K."

"And that big . . ."

"He's back in Chicago. I called to thank you."

"Young 'un, I'm almost as pleased as you are. Times like these, we forget there's a sun up there. Now tell me. You need anything? Don't lie to me. I see kids like you movin' through these yards every day. You probably haven't eaten a piece of meat for a year. You're probably starved and probably frozen and probably broke. Like darn near everyone else."

"We're O.K. We'll make it. Thanks, Mr. Stevenson."

"You see? Manners ain't around much these days. I don't mean manners. I mean . . . how many kids would take the time to call and thank someone for doin' what anyone would do?"

"Not just anyone would have done it. You did."

"Hell's bells, you need anything, you have my number. Now you go and get some food inside you."

"Yessir. Good-bye, Mr. Stevenson."

"Good-bye, William. You say hello to your sister and your little brother. You keep hold of my number. And William, when you're older, when things have gotten better—and I'll give you a little info here: Things can't get much worse—you come see me. Is that a deal, William?"

"That's a deal, Mr. Stevenson."

The prediction is that by midnight the temperature will be five to ten degrees below zero.

We are within three blocks of our basement room.

"Deirdre?"

My grunt is muffled behind my scarf.

"Deirdre?"

"Yeah, Willy?"

"Would you call it home? Our basement, I mean."

Herbie, walking in between us, cries out. He doesn't wait to hear my answer. He starts running. He's at the basement door when we arrive, waiting.

* * *

Two wooden crates nailed together serve as a table. The surface is covered with cans of sardines, boxes of crackers, cartons of milk, bags of fig newtons. There is seven cents left in the kitty.

It is as if Lackawanna never left. Until midnight, when we all give in to fatigue. The furnace is working, thanks to Carl's magic hands. The warmth is almost as gratifying as the food. Heavy lidded, heavy footed, we settle on our mattresses. The mattress on which Norman always slept remains empty. It is next to the furnace, of course. Had Norman had his way, it would have been on top of the furnace. The mattress Herbie and I share is next to Norman's.

"Deirdey, I want to sleep on Norman's mattress."

I want to say, "But what if Norman comes in?" or "But where will Norman sleep?" I certainly can't keep up the pretense much longer. And so I end up saying nothing. I try to convince myself that I am not being punished, that Herbie is not saying to me, "We'll never be close again."

"O.K., Herbie, if that's what you want."

He spreads the coats and jackets and crawls beneath them. I pull and push the pillow Herbie once used and slip an arm about it.

"Good night, Herbie. I'm glad you're back."

Is the response delayed because he is asleep or

because he no longer wants or needs to return my love? Please, Herbie, please.

"Night, Deirdey. I'm glad, too."

My heart, my soul, begin to sing.

Everyone, still luxuriating in the warmth, has returned from the streets. We have managed to beg a total of forty-seven cents.

Slezak, who no longer performs his push-ups and never shadow-boxes, dreams aloud about the coming spring. "Maybe I'll go out to California. I got an uncle out there somewhere raises oranges."

Carl argues that oranges are better than grapefruit but not as good as apples. "You ever hear anyone say, 'An orange a day keeps the doctor away'?"

Willy promises once more what he promises at least once a day to himself and to us: "I'm going back to school. Clear through college. My brother Ward always wanted me to go to college."

Slezak has fallen asleep. So has Carl, who, an hour earlier, had recited from memory the first chapter of *The Three Musketeers*. Tomorrow night he'll recite the second chapter.

"Deirdey?"

"Yeah, Herbie?"

"How'd Norman die?"

I try to sit up, but my strength has melted away. Willy, dear Willy, please come to my rescue. He doesn't.

"He froze to death, Herbie."

"Where?"

"In Chicago."

I can hear Herbie. Is he sobbing?

"Norman would have believed me."

I remember our move to Willy's tin shack in Hoover Valley. I remember Herbie whispering in my ear: "We have to bring Norman; we can't go without Norman. He's my best friend, Deirdey."

I bury my face in my pillow while hugging Herbie's old pillow to my heart.

Herbie turns to face the furnace. He begins to hum and then to sing a song my father composed, the song Norman especially loved. I roll over on my back. I sit up. I join my little brother in the melody. We sing, the two of us, of moons shining on lakes and swans floating in silvery moonlight and red roses tossed on the water by star-crossed lovers.

Is Willy sleeping? It doesn't matter. I reach out and find Herbie's hand. "Why are you awake?"

"He was kind to me."

Thinking he means Norman, I bring Herbie's hand my lips. I try to find words to say, *He was kind to me, too, Herbie. I loved him, Herbie, I loved Norman.*

"He gave me food and candy and he talked to me. He never did anything mean to me. Not once. He was always kind. He made hot chocolate for me. He read *Treasure Island* to me, and *Robinson Crusoe.*"

I clutch at the silence, grope for words, for thoughts, even for emotions. My heart sits in my chest like a hot rock.

"He said I was just like his son, Jason. Same size, same age. Jason had freckles, too."

I press my hands against my mouth.

"His son, Jason, died two years ago. On New Year's Eve. Jason needed medicine and they didn't have money and he couldn't find a job and Jason died. He wanted me to stay with him forever. I wanted to stay. I would have. He never did anything but nice things for me. Deirdey, I sang him Poppa's songs and he learned them and sang them back to me."

In the morning we go out to tramp through the snow in search of pennies and, if we're lucky, food.

Herbie, it's going to take me a while. I need time.

IV

Epilogue

Epilogue

If I can find my mother or my sister, Herbie might be his old joyous self again. I leave him with Willy and go search the old neighborhood.

The marble steps leading up to the front door are covered with snow. When we lived here, the steps, even in the meanest winter storms, were always swept clean by my mother.

I go up the stairs to 4C and ring the bell. A man opens the door. He wears no shoes or socks. The tops of his flat-tipped toes are covered with bunions. The once-white undershirt covers only the top half of his paunch. The lower half looks like an oversized, overripe tomato about to burst.

"I ain't buyin'," he says.

"I'm not selling anything. I used to live here."

"You? When?"

"A year ago."

"What's your name?"

"Callahan."

"Yeah, we used to get mail for Callahan."

"Can I have it?"

"We give it back. We've been here six months. The toilet leaks. Did the toilet leak when you lived here?"

"My sister and mother were living here when I left. Do you know where she went?"

"Nope. She wasn't here when we came six months ago. Ask Mrs. Shipley in 5A. She's been here since Moses brought down the tablets. She knows everything. Too much, in fact."

I climb the stairs and knock on the door of 5A.

"Leave it at the door," a crackling old voice calls from inside.

"Mrs. Shipley, can I talk to you? I'm Deirdre Callahan. I haven't been here for a year. We lived—"

The door leaps open. "I know where you lived. You lived in 4C. You and your brother run off." Mrs. Shipley has the craggy face and warped body of a witch; she even has a wart at the tip of her nose.

Her voice sounds as if it's filtered through sandpaper.

The kids in the building used to tease her. On Halloween we played tricks on her. My father swore that when he first met her, the day he and my mother moved into the building, she was a big woman. She is shorter than I am now.

"Where have you been? Where's your little brother? What's his name? Henry?"

"Herbie."

"I wouldn't have recognized you. Look at you. You used to be so neat. Hair combed, face washed, ribbons in your hair. Look at you. You look like a bum. Want some crackers?"

"No, thanks. I just . . . Do you know where my sister went? She was still in 4C when I left."

"She went off and married a man so handsome it made you cry to look on him. Rich, too, I hear. Happy? She went outa here all smiles and songs. How's little Henry?"

"Herbie. He's O.K. Mrs. Shipley, do you remember my mother?"

"Of course I remember your mother. Whatta you think, you think I'm addled? I remember your father, too. A prince of a man. Used to take out my garbage. Your sister came and got her and took her off like a princess, in a car. They said he had money. They were right."

I am halfway down the stairs.

"Where you goin'? You bring Henry back here for a visit. I'll give him some crackers."

On the fourth floor I see the tomato man still standing in the doorway of 4C. He's grinning, having, no doubt, overheard the entire conversation with Mrs. Shipley, who is still talking, shouting. "You Callahans was good neighbors. New people ain't like you. They eat boiled cabbage all the time. They stink the whole place up."

The tomato-paunched man puts his thumb to his nose and waves his fingers at the ceiling.

I continue to hear Mrs. Shipley from the second-floor landing. "You bring Henry by. I've got fresh crackers."

Outside were the marble steps on which Herbie and my sister, Patricia, who was never considered a golden angel, and my father and my mother used to sit on summer evenings. Now, sitting on those marble steps, scorning the snow, I lean back against a pillar.

At noon, near Times Square, Herbie walks slowly through falling snow, his song like the fine chimes of a silver bell. I follow closely behind him, my right hand on his shoulder. The sockets of both of my eyes are milky white.

A coin drops into my tin bucket. Another coin. And another.

Herbie, frozen puffs of breath suspended before his face, sings out, "Thank you, ma'am. Thank you."

Willy stands in the doorway of a deserted shop. On a cardboard box before him are four candy bars. Printed in pencil on a wrinkled brown bag is: *5¢— candy — 5¢.*

If Willy sells all four candy bars, Lackawanna will make a profit of twenty cents, because the candy cost us nothing. A woman wearing a fox around her throat gave them to Herbie yesterday. She actually gave him ten, but last night each member of Lackawanna ate one. Herbie placed a single bar on Norman's mattress. He slept on my mattress. No one will ever sleep on Norman's mattress again, we vowed, and no one will ever eat that candy bar.

The sun has been shining for several days. The snow that had turned to slush is now gone. A man dashing by, wheeling a barrel of fish, calls out, "An Indian summer day." He stops, lets his wheelbarrow down, digs in his pocket, and drops several coins and then a fish into the tin bucket.

"Thank you, thank you."

Herbie and I stroll on, singing of moons shining

on lakes and swans floating in silvery moonlight and red roses tossed on the water by star-crossed lovers. My eyes are rolled up into my head. I am weeping, not in sadness but in joy. My right hand rests on the left shoulder of my brother. Tonight I will tell him about Patricia and Momma. Tomorrow we'll start looking for them. I know we'll find them. I don't just hope it, I know it. Lackawanna went halfway across the United States to find Herbie and we found him, didn't we? Listen. Listen to Herbie's beautiful song.

About the Author

CHESTER AARON is the author of many novels for children and young adults, among them GIDEON, DUCHESS, and OUT OF SIGHT, OUT OF MIND. He received his B.A. from the University of California at Berkeley and his M.A. from San Francisco State University. Mr. Aaron is currently a professor at Saint Mary's College and lives in Occidental, California.

DATE DUE
